THE TRUTH
IN THE LIE

Further excursions into the lives of others

By Mark Swain

The Truth in The Lie
Further excursions into the lives of others

by
Mark Swain
http://markswain-author.blogspot.co.uk

Published in 2014 by
Tinderbox Publishing Limited

This book is a work of Fiction.

ISBN 978-0-9572002-3-4

Editing by Alex Swain
Cover photograph by Fumiko Jin
Cover design by Caleb Simmons
http://www.calebsimmons.co.uk

Dedication

For my children, Alexandra, Sam and Scarlett, who used to ask me to make-up stories for them. It helped me to hone my storytelling skills and gave me an immediate, sometimes uncomfortable sense of what worked and what didn't.

.

CONTENTS

Foreword

Children are natural fantasists. Once we reach adulthood, however, we are generally expected to stay within the realms of what adults accept as the real world. As a child, I remember this realisation saddening me. The world of make-believe needed to be left behind. Embellished or made up stories were called lies. Instead of being known for having lively imaginations, children like me were called liars. I learned to live with it, but anger and resentment fermented inside.

Many adults exaggerate. Relating a story to others at a social occasion, a little poetic license often makes things sound more interesting, or illustrates a point. Done well it can be a useful skill. Sometimes, however, these stories flow over the boundary into the realms of fiction – especially where alcohol is involved. Before the storyteller knows it they find themselves entwined in the uncomfortable fantasy they have woven. This reassures me. Someone's true nature is trying to break out. In Orwellian terms they are fighting back against a controlling society – sticking it to the man. Yet how fictional are these invented stories really?

In every invented story, there is a powerful truth trying to make itself known. It is this that preoccupies me. The subtlety required in order to reveal a hint of the truth, enough to enter the mind of the reader at a subliminal level. It is a constant challenge, but I can think of little that I regard as so compelling or worthwhile.

Red Card

"Dear Mr Carmichael, after repeated requests for payment of your outstanding debt to us, Dreamcar Finance Ltd hereby notifies you, that action will now be taken to recover the vehicle, blah blah, fekin' blah!"

Pat nearly always read his letters aloud to himself. Without it the contents just didn't seem to sink in. He stood staring at the letter, smelling it, examining it as a forensic scientist might.

"As a gesture of goodwill on Dreamcar Finance's part, we offer you one final opportunity of returning the vehicle to our offices by 5pm on Friday 22nd January and thereby avoiding further costs of £2,500, which will otherwise be added to your debt, this being the charge for recovery. Dreamcar Finance reserves the right... blah blah, yeah thanks a million, ya bloody shysters!"

A kettle began delivering a boiling warning from the kitchenette. Screwing the paper into a tight ball, Pat tossed it into the air as he went. A casual sideways nod caught the ball to the left side of his forehead. The crowd gasped as he raised his left foot behind him, caught the ball on his heel and sent it via a beautiful arc into the open fireplace. They screamed with delight as the flames consumed the ball. Making his entrance into the kitchenette, Pat Carmichael produced his trademark celebratory gesture of blowing smoke from a two-fingered revolver. Holstering the imaginary weapon, he removed the screaming kettle.

"Ach you've still got it, sure you have, Pat Carmichael!"

Pat Carmichael had once been a wiry, balletic footballer, according to media commentary of four years or so ago. If he still had it, nobody wanted it. Four years of living on pies and pints since his wife and kids left had turned him into a heavy slob of a man. Balletics were out of the question now. But it was his mind that had really suffered. Used to living the highlife and receiving the constant adulation of fans on account of his skills and Irish good looks, Pat had not seen this coming. He'd had a few injuries in his time, who hadn't? But nothing that a bit of physio and a week with his feet up couldn't solve. Okay, like all footballers he knew it was a short career, but at 27 retirement had seemed some way off yet. The fact was, plenty of other players had knee cartilage problems sorted out with a small keyhole operation these days, but not him. He still woke up sweating in the night, with the words of the surgeon echoing inside his head:

"I'm afraid to tell you, Mr Carmichael, that you will always walk with a limp. As for playing football, you must learn to accept that those days are entirely behind you."

Pat had never believed the surgeon. What did a bloody surgeon know about football? He had an almost God-given ability with a ball, people said. Even rival managers had said so. You couldn't take that away. Yet despite Pat's assurances that he would be back, nobody really believed it. Their faith in the former star disappeared almost overnight. It wasn't long before people didn't even remember him when he mentioned his name.

It was the same story with his wife, really. She remembered his name alright, but somehow Sandra seemed different towards him from the moment the surgeon made his pronouncement. As if he were not the same person. When she left a couple of months later, she was matter-of-fact about it.

"I fell in love with Pat Carmichael the footballer," she said, handing him the front door keys. "I'm not interested in being married to Pat Carmichael the unemployed drunk with sick in his beard."

*

At first, Pat had been sure something would turn up. The luck of the Irish, he thought. He had always been lucky, he kept reminding himself. The kids had seemed sad, but maybe for the same reasons as Sandra.

Cancelling the annual winter trip to Disneyworld in Florida had seemed more of a loss to them than not having their dad around. But that was kids for you, he had told himself. Sandra, the day she left, said she had seen a solicitor. Of course she had, she was her mother's daughter. Her mother had been married five times and had come out better off on every occasion. She was going to have the London flat, she said, and he could keep the Liverpool house. That made sense. She had never liked living in the north. The north had never liked her much either. More importantly, the Chelsea flat was paid for and the Liverpool place was in negative equity. That was gone now. It hadn't taken the bank long to foreclose. Sandra could learn a thing or two from that bank manager. "Fek'n asshole!" he muttered.

Sitting down at the breakfast bar, Pat blew on his tea. It was too hot. The milk was sour. Fortunately he'd checked the smell before he poured any in because he didn't have any more tea bags. Swearing under his breath he shovelled in another spoonful of sugar. He had always hated black tea. Looking down though, he saw he had spilled sugar onto the floor. Now it would be crunchy when he walked on it.

"You bastard!" he hissed.

There was hardly any point sweeping it up, he told himself. The apartment was shite and he knew it. Apartment? Who the hell was he kidding? It was a bloody bed-sit. You couldn't swing a cat, as his grandma used to say. Every time he walked in the door, back from another solitary session at the pub, or from pacing the streets at night when he couldn't sleep, his heart sank. It was offensive to him. In fact it was driving him off his head.

"Like living in some kind of bloody self-catering asylum!" he snapped, getting up and pouring cold water into his tea. There was a crunch from under his feet as if to torment him.

It was true. It looked like the kind of dismal place where they put people after psychiatric treatment, supposedly to reintegrate them into society.

Pat slurped his tea, the way Sandra had always told him not to. At least he could do as he liked now, he told himself, he'd had it all in his lifetime. The best and the worst of it. He had nothing now. In fact he had less than nothing. If his creditors could have made some money out of cutting up his body and selling off the parts, they would have. That's what he had told the barman at The Grapes last night. He considered it again now for a moment. Getting one of those thugs in the Railway Tavern to cut him up and post his body parts to his list of creditors. The building society, the bank, the credit cards, the corner shop, the gas, the electric, British fekin' Telecom, the Clerk to the Justices, Sandra and Dreamcar fekin' Finance, to name but a few.

"Come to think of it," he muttered to himself, "I might not have enough body parts to go round!"

Anyway that was Plan-B. Tempting as it was, right now Plan-A seemed a better option.

Plan-A had come to Pat as a result of an overheard conversation at the Railway Tavern last week. A couple of street-wise shysters in cashmere overcoats, tongues loosened by Jameson's, had been talking about a place in Rotterdam that bought prestige cars for cash and no questions asked. Porsches were particularly popular, he had heard them say. Fortunately they had also let go the name and location of the car-parts dealer who fronted this business. From what he overheard, they shipped the cars to China. All he had to do this morning was draw out the two-thousand quid he had in a building society account in his son's name, then he could say goodbye to all this and drive away to a new life.

Sipping at his revolting cup of tea, Pat looked across at the small holdall, waiting there, packed on the bed. It contained all he wanted to take with him to his new life. He sighed. He ought to be feeling more up-beat really. And why had he bothered to make the bed, he wondered? Had he felt guilty that he would be leaving without paying the rent? Memories of his poverty-stricken childhood in Ireland perhaps, moving from place to place with a drink-dependent mother? That was enough of a memory to depress anyone. He had vowed he would never get like that. Perhaps he would leave the cash for the landlord, he told himself. But he knew he wouldn't.

*

The woman behind the counter seemed suspicious, Pat thought. He had his story prepared though. All he needed to do was stick to it. It was his money anyway, he reminded himself. It was not as if he was stealing it.

Turning his face away, Pat quickly went through the key points in his head, just in case they asked. Not that they had before, but anyway. He was taking the money out to buy his son a piano. His son had begun lessons and was showing great promise. He needed to play the proud father. Under no circumstances would he panic. It was his money and he was entitled to it. He had to keep reminding himself of that.

"How would you like the money, Mr Carmichael, said the woman?"

Pat went to speak but faltered. "Sorry, I…sorry, what did you say, I don't understand?"

"How would you like the money? In which denominations? Twenties, fifties or a mixture perhaps?"

Pat stood silent and transfixed. He did want to speak, but... The woman looked puzzled. Maybe she was considering calling her manager over. He was messing it up. He'd better act quickly, he decided.

"Oh, ah, I see yes, well a mixture would be good," the words spilled out suddenly, like the sugar had that morning onto the kitchen floor. That would be the Landlord's problem now – or it would be if he could sort his game out! Pat wiped his mouth nervously.

"Sure, that's fine, yeah 'course why not, a mixture if that's okay with you?"

The woman looked down at the passbook again and then looked up at Pat. His stomach churned. For a moment he thought he might actually wet himself. Flashing through his mind was a time in a headmaster's office when he was nine. Someone had written something on a toilet wall and another boy had said it was Carmichael who had done it.

"You are the very epitome of a filthy wretch, Carmichael!" the Headmaster had told him. "If it were within my power, I would have you removed from this school."

At the time he had thought the Head said epiphany and he had worried about what the priest called "damnation."

"That's a thousand pounds in fifties, five hundred in twenties and five hundred in tens, Mr Carmichael. That leaves sixteen pounds of accrued interest."

She placed the money in a brown envelope and seemed to spend an age fiddling with the tuck-in part. Pat stared at the package. It was nearly three years since he had seen that much money. To think, he once used to earn nearly five times that amount every week, he reminded himself. Pat took it gingerly, half expecting her to snatch it back as he put his hand through the gap under the window.

Not forgetting to pick up his holdall and thank the cashier, Pat limped out into the street. He didn't dare to look back. His body wanted to run but he knew, even if his knee held-out, it would arouse suspicion. He was sure the staff must all be standing there at the window watching him.

Pat kept his hand in his jacket pocket all the way to the yard where his car was parked. He couldn't stop fingering that wad of cash. It made him nervous, but every now and then he allowed himself a smile. At one point he even broke into uncontrolled laughter, causing a bunch of schoolgirls to call after him.

"Hey perv,' yer bloody cracked you are!"

Pat had not been able to afford to run the Porsche for some time. It had been a struggle to afford the fourteen quid a month he paid a bloke to keep it in a shed, but he hadn't been able to part with her. Not when he would have got nothing back but a demand for the rest of the money he owed. Selling her for cash and pocketing maybe forty or fifty grand was a different matter. He could live on that for a long time. At least until his luck changed.

It had not occurred to him until now, but as Pat put the key in the shed door he had a terrifying sense that the car would not be there. Sick to his stomach, he hesitated with the key in the lock before turning it. He had been there only last Friday, sitting in her, smelling the leather and listening to that gorgeous engine note as he ran her to top-up the battery. But something in his water told him she had gone. Numb and with a sense of impending despair, Pat turned the key and pushed the door open. A tingling sensation ran through his body. A shortness of breath. There was nothing – nothing he could do if she had gone. But no, there she sat, gleaming red paintwork showing through the white cotton sheet. He pressed the key-fob. "That's my beauty," he murmured, as she bleeped and flashed her indicators.

"Thank Christ for that!"

Pat was not by nature a pessimist – far from it. Yet all the way down to Folkestone he was expecting something to go wrong. Was the petrol gauge misreading? Would he get a puncture? Had he forgotten his passport? What was that clicking sound? Was that a police car following him? He pulled over several times on the way down to reassure himself. Finally, with a huge sense of relief, he found himself checking-in at the Eurotunnel terminal and being waved forward into a queue by a scruffy looking man in a high-viz vest. Okay so far he thought, but surely he would be stopped and questioned by immigration? Yet no, after a short wait he followed the other vehicles onto the ramp. Soon he felt the comforting rumble of the train making its way through the dark towards France.

*

"Freedom!" Pat shouted as he drove down the ramp onto French tarmac. He punched the air with a sense of triumph that he hadn't felt since the hat-trick he had scored four years ago against Tottenham at Whitehart Lane. That third goal, sending the fans wild and his team into the European Cup, had been the peak of his footballing career. Back then he had thought there would be plenty more triumphs like that still to come, yet only a month later it was all over. He hadn't deserved that, after all the effort he had put in to get there. No point in living in the past though, he told himself. In this new life he felt sure that the balance was about to be redressed. His luck was on the change. It was the Pat Carmichael of old who blew the smoke from his imaginary gun after driving through the first immigration barrier.

"Your passport s'il vous plait monsieur," said the man by the second barrier.

Pat, still pumped-up and smiling, handed the official his passport and waited patiently. He might take the autoroute to Rotterdam, he thought, despite the extra cost. Floor-it a bit on the way. One last day of fun before he sold her.

"Merci Monsieur," said the man, handing back the passport and gesturing for Pat to proceed.

Pat gave the throttle a blip and pulled off. There was a throaty roar and a slight wheel-spin. Seeing another official step out from one of the customs sheds, he cursed himself. The man waved him towards the inspection area.

"Serves you right Carmichael, you fek'n boy racer," Pat laughed.

In the inspection area a uniformed woman stepped forward and asked for Pat's passport. Pat smiled. It was the kind of smile he had used with women back when he was at the top of his game. She smiled back.

"Sorry, it's hard to resist giving a car like this a bit of welly when you set off," he said coolly. It was all he could do to resist calling her sweetheart.

"I'm sure it is," replied the woman.

There was something about French women when they spoke English, Pat thought. He wondered what time she got off work.

"Could you please to open the trunk," said the woman pointing to the back of the car.

"I keep the engine in that one," laughed Pat. "The trunk's at the front. Same as an elephant."

Pat flipped the bonnet lever and jumped out quickly to lift it for her. The trunk was empty but for an emergency triangle. Pat's holdall was on the passenger seat. The woman thanked him and Pat went to close the bonnet.

"Not yet please!" said the woman.

The woman turned and waved to a colleague, who came out of a cabin leading a brown Labrador.

"Lovely dog," said Pat.

"He is young and a little naughty," replied the woman. "We have sometimes to be strict with him."

"Sounds a bit like me!" laughed Pat.

The woman smiled and looked at Pat sideways. He

felt sure he was getting somewhere with her. Perhaps he would leave it until tomorrow to go to Rotterdam. He risked a crafty wink before she turned away. Meanwhile, encouraged by the handler, the Labrador had jumped into bonnet space and began sniffing about excitedly.

"Ilya quelque chose dessous?" asked the handler.

"Ah, do you have something under?" asked the woman.

"Just tools and the spare wheel," said Pat.

"Show me please," she said, gesturing with her gloved hand.

Pat stepped forward and lifted the cover to reveal, not only a spare wheel but a plastic carrier bag along with a separate smaller bag containing, it transpired, some form of white powder. Rummaging with its nose, the dog barked loudly and wagged its tail. Pulling the dog back, the handler placed his hand in his pocket and handed the dog a treat.

"What the…!" spluttered Pat, in horror.

"Something more than a spare wheel and tools I think," said the woman. "Stand away from the car please. Perhaps you will take a seat in the office."

Pat was shaking now. How on earth drugs had got into the boot of his car he had no idea. Drugs had never been his style. Yes he had enjoyed the odd puff on a joint now and then when he was a spotty youth but nothing more. So much for a new life, he thought to himself, this was a nightmare come true. "Your luck's changed all right now Pat Carmichael," he muttered to himself. "Changed for the feking worse mate!"

Pat wracked his brains. Who could have put drugs in his car, he asked himself? Either it had to be someone like the guy who owned the shed, thinking it was a safe hiding place, or it was someone who had a grudge against him. It must be.

Looking through the portacabin office window, Pat could see a collection of officials standing around his precious car, beginning to take her apart. The woman who had initially dealt with him was walking towards the office. The door opened.

"So Mr Carmichael, is there anything you want to tell us?"

"Tell you? N...no not really. Only that I'm innocent. I never put those drugs in that boot, n...no way!"

"I am rather hoping you could save us the trouble to taking your car apart, Mr Carmichael. I would like you to tell us if there are anything hidden some other places in the car."

The woman was serious, but she seemed to have a hint of a smirk trying to break through. He knew her type, he thought, they take pleasure in seeing people in this situation.

"Uhm. Well... the car's been parked up for quite a

while you see," said Pat, aware that he was shaking. "In… in a big lock-up I rent off a guy down Kennington way – near where I've been living. I've been, you know, going and running her engine once a week like. If… well, if anyone had, you know, messed with her… Well…" Pat was running out of ideas. "Well what I'm trying to say is that I think I'd have noticed."

"So when did you last look in the trunk, Mr Carmichel?"

"Pff, I dunno. Probably a couple of years ago I'd say. It's hard to remember."

"Do you perhaps play sport, Mr Carmichael?"

"I used to," said Pat, brightening up.

But any ideas of impressing her with tales of him being a professional footballer were probably not going to help him, he thought. More likely that they'd see drugs as going hand in hand with a footballer's life, more like. Images of prison were more in his thoughts now. No doubt they had been on the phone and knew everything about him, he told himself. It would be goodbye car, goodbye new life and goodbye freedom.

"I was a footballer. Professional like. Played for Fulham." Pat hung his head. "All over now, thanks to my knee."

"Hmm, would you come back to the car please," said the woman, opening the door.

The other officials seemed to have stopped searching. They were stood casually around the car now. The bonnet was still up as the woman beckoned Pat to follow her.

"This is your things for football?" she asked.

Laid out on a folding table next to the car was a grubby Fulham shirt and an equally filthy pair of shorts. Seeing the shirt sent a shudder down his spine. The socks and his jock strap seemed to have partially disintegrated and the smell was not at all welcoming.

"These things were in the bag Mr Carmichael," said the woman. "They are yours?"

"Uhm, well, yes," replied Pat, uncomfortably, they are mine, yes."

"And this bag of white powder – this is yours also?"

"Well n…no. No way. I don't do drugs. Never have!"

"Nobody says anything about drugs, Mr Carmichael," said the woman sternly, "this is washing powder."

"W… washing powder?" mumbled Pat.

"Yes. What did you think?" replied the woman. "But these clothes. You cannot take them into France unless you wash them. They are a serious hygiene problem, you know. Our laboratory have tested them and they find more than two-thousand type of dangerous bacteria!"

Pat stood looking at the woman in disbelief. What

was happening here, he wondered? One by one the other officials began chuckling. The woman herself could resist smiling no longer. Soon they were all in fits of laughter.

"Hah! You can keep them if you like," said Pat, nervously, "or burn them if you have to!"

Putting on a pair of latex gloves, the woman delicately began returning Pat's moulding kit to the bag. Following this she put it into a new, clean bag and placed it back into the boot. One of the other officials closed the bonnet and handed Pat the keys.

"You may go on your way now," said the woman, "but you should stop to a laundry in Calais, monsieur or put them into the fire. Bon voyage, Monsieur Carmichael, and welcome to France."

Greta

After a long day's ride from Budapest, we arrived at a river and had to wait half an hour to cross on what we were told was a floating bridge. This revealed itself to be a flat-bottomed boat with an outboard that crossed every hour. In between times, a lazy boatman sat on the rail of the boat, fishing with a long stick and a short piece of line tied to the end. With nothing better to do while we waited, I wondered about what was on the end of the line. It occurred to me he might have a bent pin with a worm on it as I used to when I was a boy, living by the river Test in Hampshire.

It seemed a long wait before the boatman roused himself and chugged across the river to collect us. Fascinated by the relaxed life this man must lead, I spoke to him as we crossed. He once worked on cargo ships sailing out of Trieste, he said, but his wife had complained about his long absences, so he had set up the floating bridge. His wife then left him, but he enjoyed the easy life so much he stuck with it. Although it seemed a menial job to us, every passenger shook hands formally with him as they disembarked, making it clear that he carried a good deal of respect in the area. He waved us off, doffing his battered captain's hat. We were nearing the town of Csongrad, he told us.

"Five kilometres more!"

By the time we cycled into town it was dark. It was not a large place but it was bustling with people heading home after work. What type of work went on here, other than that of the boatman or the people we saw stripping maize, I could not guess.

After asking a number of people for help, we managed to get ourselves directed to the only accommodation in the area – a hotel. Arriving at the large old building we lifted a heavy brass ring that pulled a cord and agitated a bell inside. The old door creaked open and revealed a pale young woman. Something about her startled us.

"Welcome to inside. Step forward please."

We thanked her and cautiously moved towards the reception, behind which sat an elderly lady. She smiled and said something in Hungarian.

"My mother does not speak the foreign languages," said the girl. "I, however, can speak English, Russian, German, French, Italian and Serbo-croat. Yes, yes, and Hungarian of course. Please have look the prices here my establishment. We have the hot water and bath.

Breakfasts will be include the price please."

We relaxed. The price seemed very fair and the old lady seemed kind, as did the somewhat cybernetic daughter.

"Orlovka!" she said abruptly, handing me a pen.

After signing the register and presenting our passports, we were led up a dark stone staircase to our room. Before opening the heavy door, the girl turned towards us and hesitated a moment.

"My name is Greta," she said, her gaze uncomfortably direct. It sounded more like a warning than a greeting.

Greta was about 20, wearing a rather fashionable tracksuit and narrow glasses, yet somehow she still managed to look like a young 1950's Soviet woman. Her fixed stare held us there stiffly for some moments. I let go of my breath, trying to relax. Greta's wide face was friendly enough, but she did not seem to smile. There was certainly something abnormal about her manner. Sinister perhaps. I wondered what might be behind the door. Eventually, one of her eyes began to twitch and she looked down. With a heavy turn of the key the door creaked open.

Timorously my son Ken and I followed Greta into a large dimly lit room. It was fitted out with what seemed to be furniture from the post-war era. A shaft of dusty light cut through a crack in the heavy curtains, giving us the sense almost that we had stepped into a part of

Hungary's past. There was a strange smell I could not quite identify. Something medicinal, perhaps. She drew back the long heavy curtains to reveal a tall window that looked down into a substantial cobbled courtyard. We noticed a pair of bikes standing against the wall and then realised that they were our own. How had they got there, I wondered? The elderly mother must have moved them, I supposed, although it seemed unlikely. Looking out onto the grand Austro-Hungarian courtyard I felt that a horse-drawn carriage, or mounted soldiers with muskets might arrive at any moment. I looked at Ken. He too looked mesmerised.

"This courtyard is quite beautiful, is not?"

Greta's words echoed in the high-ceilinged room and it was a moment or two before I realised it was she who had spoken. Pulling myself together, I turned to look at her. The full sun on her face had revealed a surprising feature – she had one brown eye and one blue. I tried not to stare. She turned and began showing us the room, opening every drawer and cupboard as if carrying out an obsessively practiced routine.

"It is a most spracious room, is not?"

"Oh, very precious, yes. Thank you," I replied.

"Yes, sorry, much space." She looked embarrassed at her minor linguistic slip. "It is our pleasure. We have few stranger guests such days. We will try hardly to give you comfort here."

"We will try hard to be good guests," smiled Ken.

There was a moment's hesitation as she turned. A change had occurred in Greta's eyes. An awkward silence descended, followed by a radiant smile. Ken had thawed her. Thank God, I thought. Maybe now we won't be tied up and held prisoner in the cellar.

Greta showed us into a large, historic bathroom. Over a long rust-stained bath was a device I had seen before, or something similar at least. My grandmother had owned one when I was small. It was known as The Geyser: a huge threatening gas boiler smelling of burning gas, that shook and gurgled when lit, threatening to explode at any moment. The fear I reserved for this monstrous device as a child, I realised, remained with me still. I had no intention of using it, nor of allowing Ken to.

The mysterious Greta had become animated and was now eager to talk, questioning us about what we had seen on our journey and what we thought of her country. She was also very informative. Sitting down at the writing desk, she began to give us a potted history of Hungary. Ken and I, meanwhile, were transformed into an attentive audience, perched on one of the beds. In addition to enlightening historical and political facts, Greta was ready to provide local information.

"Now, I want to commend you about a very good pizza restaurant near to this establishment," she said. "It is very marvellous."

A pizza restaurant did not sound particularly marvellous to me – commended or not. We were to find later, however, that it was the only eating establishment in town. Reluctantly, hunger did lead us there, only to discover it did indeed serve excellent pizza. More surprising though were the furnishings and the exquisitely prepared Hungarian dishes consisting of very fresh fish and delicious wild game from the surrounding forests. The staff here also seemed entirely out of place. The elderly waiter was dressed in black trousers and a stiffly starched white jacket with gold braided epaulettes. He was reminiscent of someone from a grand Monte Carlo hotel in the aristocratic opulence of the 1920's. It added to the sinister atmosphere we had felt pervaded the town since we arrived.

As the lid was lifted on another large silver terrine, this time containing an enormous bird that could only have been a peacock or a small ostrich, it all started to feel rather hard to believe. I glanced out of a window, across the road at the hotel and saw the old woman's face disappear behind a twitching curtain. The waiter followed my gaze and sighed.

"Yes, you should to be careful my friends."

"The old lady?" I asked.

"No, no, young girl. Old mother is dead."

The man crossed himself several times.

"Dead?" I asked, confused.

"No old mother now. She is dead five years before. In the river. They say accident but everybody don't think.

23

Be most careful." He crossed himself again.

"Greta?" I asked.

There was a crash as the waiter dropped the lid onto the terrine. He looked down at me.

"Better don't to speak her name, my friend."

All In Good Time

"I can get on with this by myself, you go and serve customers," said Anita.

Anita had been working at the café since Monday. Surely Glenda could see by now that she could make a bacon sandwich without supervision?

"I'm sorry Anita but I have to watch," said Glenda, awkwardly.

"It's a bacon sandwich, Glenda, what's there to watch?"

"It's not that I doubt your ability, Anita. It's part of the new procedures I agreed."

"What, that you need to watch every grain of food being prepared? Honestly, you haven't taken your eyes off me for the last four days. Surely you've sussed by now that I know what I'm about?"

"There's history behind it Anita. Sorry."

"History? What do you mean by history?"

"Nothing, just that things have happened in the past that mean I have to watch while everything's prepared."

"So in other words you don't trust me?"

"I didn't say that."

"What is it then?"

"It's more that I can't risk trusting anyone. That's why we have the new procedure."

"Oh. And do you mind me asking what brought on this new procedure, Glenda?"

"I'd rather not say, if you don't mind, but it's nothing to do with you personally, Anita, I can say that much."

"Well I'm sorry Glenda, that's not good enough. Either you tell me what it's about or I'll take my wages and go. I don't think that's unreasonable."

Glenda clasped her head in frustration.

"Look Anita, this is not easy for me either. It's not exactly a secret or anything. I mean I could tell you, but you'd have to keep it to yourself... Actually, I suppose that does make it a secret."

Anita made a zipping gesture with her lips.

"Okay. The offices over the road?" said Glenda.

"The Environmental Health Offices?"

"Yes. Except that the fourth floor is not Environmental Health. Not really."

"Who is it?"

Glenda looked over her shoulder, then took a biro out of her top pocket and wrote on a waiter's pad. Anita looked over while the tomato ketchup bottle remained suspended in mid-air above the sandwich. Turning her head on one side she read it. MI-6, it said. Glenda tore it into thin strips and put them quickly into the bin.

"And what?" whispered Anita, theatrically. "Where's the connection with my cooking?"

"Isn't it obvious?" whispered Glenda. "Poisoning. They moved here from Westminster after one of their 'opos' got taken out. Apparently they traced it back to a sandwich bar opposite their old offices. A temp the shop had taken on, he said. She disappeared the same day. Vanished. She had an East European accent, he said."

"He?" said Anita. "Who's he?"

"A man came in before they moved there. He'd been in for tea a few times and… Well you know, I'd noticed something about him. I don't know… the way he kept watching me. Well, blow me if he didn't come and have a word. It was at the end of the day. I was just locking up and he said he needed to take me over the road for a vetting appointment."

"He what?"

"Yes I know! He sat me in a room for three hours and questioned me. It was amazing really. Like, you know, on TV. They seemed to know every detail about me and my family going back years, down to what newspaper my granddad read. Anyhow, we get plenty of business from them over there is the other point. We don't want to lose that. But I'm sure they've got surveillance on us. I mean they would have, wouldn't they?"

"Well yes of course Glenda, they do that don't they? It's on the telly!" Anita smirked.

"It's a serious matter, Anita." Glenda was still whispering.

"You know perhaps it is," said Anita. "We could check."

Glenda put down the glass she was polishing. "What d'you mean, check?"

*

Glenda was folding paper napkins when Anita arrived the following morning.

"Das Vidanya," said Anita, loudly.

"What's that?" replied Glenda, with a quizzical stare.

"Sorry, it was a slip. My Grandfather used to say it instead of good morning. I think he was from St Petersburg. An avid reader of The Morning Star now I come to think of it."

Anita poured herself a cup of tea then went to sit in the window. Glenda was watching her with interest. Delving into her bag, Anita took out a newspaper and began reading.

"The bakery man's late this morning," said Glenda.

"I noticed," said Anita, smiling. "I notice everything."

Soon after that, the baker's van pulled up outside and Anita put her newspaper back into her bag. Slipping on her overall, she made her way outside to help carry in the trays to the kitchen. She was aware of Glenda's eyes following her and she wondered how long it would be before she was tempted to check her bag.

Surprisingly for a Friday, it developed into a busy day and Glenda was hard pushed to watch all the food preparation at the same time as serving customers. Exasperated, Anita shook her head in disbelief. By three o'clock though, things had calmed down and Glenda sent Anita for a break.

Anita was entitled to at least one break. She had become accustomed to taking this in the park on the corner and sometimes calling in at the library. During today's break heavy rain began to fall. Glenda assumed Anita had been held up as a result of the rain – at the library perhaps – but when she had still not returned by four o'clock, she telephoned her mobile. A backlog of orders was building up. She was obviously on her way,

Glenda told herself, since there was no reply. Another frantic hour passed, but still there was no sign of Anita.

"Funny, she's usually so punctual," Glenda said to herself.

The majority of lunchtime customers had limited time within which to get some lunch. Seeing the café was short staffed most had now decided to go elsewhere. Glenda was not entirely sorry to see them go today. Eventually the tables were empty apart from an elderly gentleman who often spent an hour over one cup of tea. Glenda was just about to sit down for a well-earned rest herself, when she noticed Anita's bag in the kitchen and thought to check whether her mobile phone had been left there. She hadn't heard it ring. Looking into the open bag she searched for a pocket but was distracted by the newspaper. There was something unusual about it. She hesitated a moment, then pulled it out. It was a foreign newspaper. The hammer and sickle against a red rectangle told her what kind of paper it was. She gasped.

"May I take that?" said a voice from behind her.

Glenda turned, to see a man in a black raincoat with a dripping umbrella. It was the man from across the road.

"She won't be coming back for it," he said.

"What's happened to her?"

"Immigration irregularity. Overstayed her visa and she has no work permit I'm afraid. As her employer you should really have checked." The man looked hard into

Glenda's eyes, then smiled. "Don't worry; you're not in trouble. Perhaps next time though, you should tell us when you take on new staff. Especially foreigners."

"But she's English," said Glenda, open-mouthed. "She's from Streatham, near where I live. I've met her sister!"

"Yes they're very good at that," said the man. "It's a double bluff. These are not amateurs you know."

The man put out his hand for the bag. Reluctantly, Glenda handed it to him.

"Thank you."

"J…just a minute," stammered Glenda, "I'm remembering now. Anita said it was an experiment. She said we should check if we were under surveillance. Come to think of it she made a big play of taking out that newspaper and waving it around near the window."

"Did she?" said the man. "Why would she do that, do you think?"

"Well that's what I'm saying." Glenda hesitated, realising she had made a blunder. "Well I had to tell her, you see. She wanted to know why I insisted on watching her preparing the food. It had become too obvious. I tried to put her off but she was about to resign. It's not as if I'm trained for all this."

"Mrs Ryan, I know this has been a bit of a shock for you. Now look, if I were to ask you to lock up your shop and come with me, how long would that take you?"

"Well... I don't know. But what have I..."

"The keys Mrs Ryan," said the man, holding out his gloved hand.

Glenda looked around the café. Fortunately there were no customers to be embarrassed in front of and only a couple of cups to go in the dishwasher. The old man in the corner seemed to have gone. She unplugged the kettle and the toaster and then switched off the lights.

"But I haven't done anything wrong," said Glenda, nervously.

"Possibly not," said the man. "I'm afraid it's a matter of geographical incompatibility, however. We can't possibly move our offices again so soon. We've exceeded our budget for the year. Now tell me; I believe you live alone, is that correct?"

Turning the open sign around to closed, Glenda hesitated before answering. "I'm a widow."

"Yes, I did remember that," said the man, examining the stitching on his gloves. "It's just that I was wondering if we might have dinner one evening. Lighten things up a bit. A film perhaps?"

Glenda stopped abruptly as they reached the corner and turned to look at him. Just at that moment, however, a van pulled up, causing her to step back against the front window. It alarmed her. Environmental Health

Department was written down the side of the van. Out of it climbed a workman in white coveralls. He seemed to know the man in the raincoat. Glenda watched as the workman placed a notice on the café window and fixed hazard tape around the building. She looked up at the notice. "Danger, contamination," it said.

"Traces of hydro-carbon related substances picked up in the water table, I believe," said the driver. "Not your fault luv. There was a garage behind you until a few years back. These places often just dump their waste oil in the ditch, down the drains, anywhere to save money. Environmental Health are very strict where food premises are concerned. We'll do some tests. We can't be too careful you see."

"B...but what about my business?" said Glenda "I have to make a living."

"We can talk about that," said the man in the raincoat. "Let's go somewhere quiet for a cup of tea. There's a place behind Debenhams."

*

Glenda couldn't see why the man – Derek he had asked her to call him – why he had chosen the small table. It was not a popular café. There were plenty of other larger tables. Some people were like that though, she reminded herself. Derek spoke quietly. No doubt that was a habit too in his job.

"Now there's no need to talk to anyone about all this, Glenda," said Derek. "Better to keep it between

33

ourselves. If anyone asks, I suggest you tell them that you closed the café to start a new life somewhere by the seaside. Retirement perhaps? Early retirement of course."

"But I can't afford to retire!" insisted Glenda.

"Well we'll see about that," said Derek, placing his gloved hand on hers. "All in good time my dear. Perhaps we could talk about it when we go out to dinner?"

Glenda glanced up at him for a moment then returned to stirring her tea. Maybe she had missed something, she thought? It had been a confusing day. Almost like a dream.

"When I was a girl," she said suddenly, "in the fifties, there was a woman lived next door to us. She was in a wheelchair. A cripple. Well, except probably not really. She lived alone, but she took in lodgers. Paying guests they called it back then – PG's. Usually for a week or so, or sometimes just a couple of nights. Anyway, I used to try to talk to the visitors – you know as kids do – but do you know what, they never said a word to me in answer. Looking back, I don't think they spoke English. I don't know exactly, but this seemed to go on for years, then one day a load of police cars came in the early hours. My brother and me got up and watched from behind the curtains. The woman in the wheelchair... well, they took her away. But do you know what? That woman walked down the front path and into the police van as bold as you like! My mum wouldn't say much about it but at school they said she was a spy and that she'd killed people. Killed her husband too, they said. Oh yes, and there was us living next door and me picking blackberries off her bush!"

"I think we should go," said Derek. He seemed uncomfortable all of a sudden. "I need to be getting back to HQ."

The man who ran the café seemed uncomfortable too, and relieved to see them leave. Glenda had left her tea. The truth was she hadn't liked the look of it. There was tea dust on the surface. The kind you get with cheap teabags. Someone said they made them from what got swept up off the factory floor. Walking back along the road to her café, Glenda watched Derek go back into the Environmental Health building. The hazard tape was still in place. It would probably do her good to stop work for a while, she thought, she needed a break.

The Crossing

At my current level of tiredness I knew I should not be driving. After three days without leaving the office and having had virtually no sleep, I was completely exhausted. Now that the crisis at the office was over I had fallen into a kind of otherworldly state. The price of prolonged caffeine abuse, I surmised. I knew I just needed to get home quickly before I collapsed. Then I could sleep for the whole weekend if I wanted to. The road was so familiar to me that I hardly needed to be awake anyway, and at 3am there was virtually no other traffic.

The lights of town appeared around the headland as I passed Iron Wharf Boatyard. Maybe this year I would find time to get that boat back in the water, I reminded myself. Then we could get our life back on track – spend some more time together, maybe some overnighters down the coast like we used to before I got my big promotion. I sighed and relaxed back into my seat. The leather squeaked. Ah, the sound of luxury, I thought to myself. Those were wonderful happy times. Nothing except a small beachfront shack, we had, and that little seventeen-foot boat, but life was great. Now we had money but no time to enjoy it.

"Jeezus!" I shouted, swerving. "What the hell was that?"

I looked around. A barefoot child in a white dress – looked like a nightdress – was standing right there in the road. What the hell was she doing out at 3am trying to wave someone down. I had only narrowly missed her. I screeched to a halt and turned again to look back. I was pretty shaken up – sick at the thought that I could have hit her. I got out of the car and looked back up the road, but there was nothing. I shuddered. There was a kind of luminous mist and a chill in the air that seemed most unusual for August.

"Bloody weird!" I thought.

Hurriedly I climbed back into the car and locked the doors. I had that feeling. The one you sometimes get where you feel sure that when you turn the key the car's not going to start. Reluctantly I turned the key and with a sense of relief, heard the engine catch. I revved her hard. Slowly, very slowly, I reversed back to where the child had been standing. Surely my mind had begun playing tricks on me, I thought? It only became apparent to me later that the child had looked strangely like my daughter Melanie.

"God I must have been hallucinating," I muttered, "there's nobody there."

I checked the time. Nearly a quarter past three. I'm not the nervous type, but I knew I needed to get home quickly before something bad happened. It was only two miles through the tunnel, then a few miles after that and I'd be there.

"Stop being ridiculous," I told myself. "You're sound. Sound!"

Instilling into myself a sense of steely determination, I put my foot down hard as I entered the tunnel. The car seemed to respond like a whipped stallion. It lifted my mood, helping me to put the fear to the back of my mind.

"Whoa yeah, and that's why I bought an Alfa!" I shouted.

Still accelerating hard, I reached for the button and opened the electric sunroof. This was better! The raucous engine note engulfed the car, magnified by the enclosed tunnel. I pushed her harder, really beginning to enjoy myself now. As the Alfa gained speed, the long straight tunnel stretching before me seemed to blur. God, I loved my life! I gripped the wheel tighter. Only the dark hole at the end was in focus, and at this moment that was all that mattered – getting to the end. The engine was singing loudly, holding that rasping racy note like a big old blues sax. I looked down at the clock. Yes I knew I shouldn't have at that speed, but I had to know if I'd hit the max.

"Bloody hell, a hundred and forty!" I shouted. "Outrageous!"

I shook my fist at the road ahead then quickly snatched back the wheel.

Relaxing back into my seat, I breathed out and focussed again on the black spot at the end of the tunnel.

"Strange," I murmured to myself, "it should be bigger by now. Surely at this bloody speed I should be through it?"

But of course it is amazing how you can lose your sense of time when you are having fun.

Unsettled somewhat, I eased up a little on the throttle and closed the roof. The noise had become deafening and my hair felt like it had been wrenched out at the roots. I glanced down again. I was still doing over a hundred, but looking back up at the end of the tunnel it still didn't seem to have got any nearer. This was bizarre. I looked at the clock on the dash. Still 03:14…at the speed I'd been going? I checked the trip meter. 166.4 miles. I accelerated again. The engine note rose and with it the wind rushed louder. My knuckles were white on the wheel. A hundred and thirty five, a hundred and forty, then creeping up to a hundred and forty-five mph. I eased off again and looked back at the clock. Crazy! Still 03:14 and still 166.4 miles. I looked once more at the end of the tunnel. It was definitely no closer. Something was very wrong here. I tried to think what could have caused it, but none of it made sense. Yes I was tired, but I had checked against the clock. I checked my wristwatch. The same time. There was no rational explanation. I had really been moving at speed, there was no doubt about that.

I was becoming panicked now. How could I get out of this, I began to ask myself? There seemed to be no point of reference except for the instruments in the car and my watch, and it seemed like they were telling me lies. Maybe there was an electrical fault, I wondered? Italian electrics are notoriously unreliable, of course, why hadn't I thought of that? Hell, if the car broke down there was no other traffic to flag down. Nothing at all had passed me. In fact, come to think of it I'd seen nobody since I got onto the coast road – nobody except that little girl. I looked in my rear-view mirror. There was nothing behind. I started to brake. At least the brakes still worked, I told myself.

Switching on the emergency flashers I pulled in close to the curb. There was still nothing in either direction so with difficulty in the narrow confines of the tunnel I turned the car around. An idea came to me. Pulling up my shirtsleeve I checked my wristwatch again: 03:14. This was bloody crazy.

"Okay, okay, so we'll go via the mountain route if the tunnel's not working," I muttered, trying to ignore the stupidity of what I was saying.

After a few minutes in that direction – and still the same time on the clocks – I could see I was getting no nearer to the end I'd entered by. I sped up again, but as expected, it made no difference. It was the same story. Obviously I was going mad.

"Not possible – not bloody possible! No way!" I screamed.

I pounded my fists on the wheel then leaned on the horn, holding it down for a good thirty seconds. I was still going nowhere, of course, but I felt a little better. I think it was at this point I accepted that I must have been imagining all this. It was the only thing that made sense. Could I be dreaming, I wondered? After all I was very tired. I pulled over again, switched on the flashers and switched off the engine. Getting out I slammed the door impatiently. What else was there to do?

"Fine, I'll bloody-well walk it then," I shouted.

The sound of my voice echoed slightly, but it was an odd, flat sound. Somehow I had hoped that hearing my own voice would make things seem more real, but the weird dull effect just made it sound like a horror film. No, there was nothing else for it now, I was shattered but I was going to have to head home on foot. Come and retrieve the car tomorrow. Probably from the car-pound, I told myself.

Taking my warm jacket and a high-visibility vest from the boot, I set off. Two miles would take about twenty minutes or half an hour, I estimated, and then once I got out of the tunnel I could call my wife to collect me. For what it was worth, I checked my watch again. 03:14. I knew that was not possible, but it was what it said. It must be the tiredness, I told myself again. I knew I just needed to get home then I'd be fine. Stepping up my pace I strode on, counting the concrete joints along the tunnel as I went.

I should say at this point that I felt sure that the change to walking and counting the joints would solve my problem. I know that sounds daft but I was very tired, remember. Well of course after about half an hour on foot, my legs ached but my watch still read 03:14 and the end of the tunnel looked no closer. It occurred to me to keep my eyes open for an emergency phone, but there was no sign of one. There was still no sign of life either. Not a car or a flash of lights, nothing. I was close to tears and just about ready to give up. And it was just then when I heard something. That welcoming sound of an engine behind me. I swung around in disbelief. Sure enough there were headlights approaching. I stood in the road waving desperately, knowing this might be my best chance of escape. As it approached I could see it was a bus and it was slowing down. It had seen me!

"Oh thank God for that, thank you so much!" I called out.

I was crying with relief, yet at the same time a nagging feeling inside told me this was too good to be true. Surely the bus was going to speed-up at the last minute and drive by, or run me down or something? But in fact it didn't. With a squeak of brakes it pulled over next to me, and the door opened. Climbing aboard I spoke to the driver. He looked kind, I remember, and pleased to help me.

"The thing is, I... I only need to get through this tunnel," I said weakly. "If you could just take me to the other end, my wife..."

"Ah, there are no interim stops I'm afraid," said the man. "We go all the way."

"All the way to where?" I asked.

"Hah, and wouldn't we all like to know that sir?" laughed the man. "It depends upon your point of view."

What did he mean, I wondered? I looked along the bus at the other passengers. They were mainly elderly and confused. Most of them looked kind of unwell, with sickly complexions. Probably an outing from a home, I thought. They stared at me blankly, all except one younger man who seemed to be making a "no, no" gesture with his finger and shaking his head. It looked like he was injured – in fact there was a nasty gash inside his hairline and blood on his jacket. I began to feel most unsure about taking this bus, and the driver sensed it.

"Please sir, you need help," he said "Take your seat – you need to come with us. Of course you may get through on your own in the end, but it'll be much easier on you if you complete the journey with the rest of us."

"But what's happened?" I asked, "What's gone wrong?"

"That's not my place to tell you, I'm afraid sir," said the driver. "Don't worry, I'm sure it'll all become clear when we get there. There's a whole team assigned to deal with post-traumatic shock."

I felt confused. Post-traumatic shock? Had there been some kind of disaster? I breathed deeply, trying to calm myself. Whatever it was that had gone wrong it did seem sensible to take the bus, and it would be easier, I could see that. I'd made no progress on my own after all. Yet things seemed to have been trying to tell me not to go this way, hadn't they? The little girl by the road who looked like Melanie? The younger man sitting over there? I needed to get home to my family, to my wife and daughter, and this bus would not be going there, I felt sure of that. In fact nobody seemed to know where in hell it was going.

"Thanks," I said, "but I think I'll walk it on my own. I need to get home to my family you see." I stepped back down off the bus.

"If you don't mind me saying so sir," called the driver, "it's rather late for that. You please yourself. But take my advice. Just be sure to keep going. Never, never give up, that's the thing. That's what they say." And at that he closed the door and drove off.

Do you know, none of the old people on the bus looked at me as that bus drove away? I tell a lie, the young man with the cut head did turn and wave, but they all seemed preoccupied with that dark point at the end of the tunnel. Just as I had been when I was driving.

Anyhow, as that bus drove off I looked down at my

watch: 06:30.

"At last," I said to myself, "things are improving! So what's to do now?"

I focussed on that point at the end of the tunnel again; only now that spot looked different. The sunrise I suppose, and a single puff of gold edged cloud. My tiredness forgotten I began running. The light provided an easier target to head for. Somehow it seemed more logical to be running towards the light than towards darkness.

Never give up, the man had said. Never, never give up. I was determined not to.

Masaji

I was talking to a guy in the canteen the other day – one of the history professors. I'd always thought of him as pretty conservative up to that moment. Anyway we were talking about the difficulties of dealing with teenage boys; coming of age, all that stuff. He started telling me about his son who had recently turned eighteen. He said he had followed his own father's example and taken his son out on the town, just the two of them. Apparently after starting off at a bar and getting him well oiled, he took his son to a brothel and paid for a pair of ladies who charged by the quarter hour. Apparently he had to bang on the door and drag his son out after an hour and a half, for fear of how high the bill was going to go. He asked me had I not thought of doing the same kind of thing with my son. I was taken aback by the suggestion.

My son and I are very close. Unavoidable really, given our experiences in China when he was younger. We went there on a trip after my wife left. I suppose we both felt abandoned and wanted to get away. We had always said we would go to China as a family, so it seemed the obvious place to go in order to lift our spirits. My son Sean had recently finished school and had been doing casual work in a restaurant. He hated the work, and I had to get away, so I took a month off from my lecturing job at the university, booked the flights, arranged the visas and off we went. The trip went well for most of that month. We visited the Great Wall, the Terracotta Army and all of that cultural "must see" stuff, but it was in the last week that things went wrong.

For the last week we had agreed to have no pre-planned agenda. When the time came we decided to take a train north then trek up into the hills of Inner Mongolia. Accommodation for tourists was almost non-existent up there but somehow after chatting to some men in a sort of makeshift bar, we found ourselves staying at a kind of cooperative farm. The people were very welcoming and loved to stay up late drinking together. Naturally we felt it incumbent on us to join them. I suppose it was a bit of a bonding opportunity for the two of us as well.

Not much farming seemed to go on at the cooperative. The residents put most of their efforts into brewing a strong local spirit. The only farming that did go on was the growing of an almost inedible turnip-like root vegetable. Fortunately this vegetable grew like a weed on their fields so demanded very little effort in cultivation.

They had tried feeding this vegetable to chickens and

goats but no animal seemed prepared to eat it. They had even tried drying it and burning it to keep warm in winter but with a similar lack of success. However, these were inventive people, who liked to party. It didn't take them too long to discover that the vegetable, after lengthy boiling, could be pulverised, brewed, and then distilled into a really powerful alcoholic drink.

So the word got around about what good hooch this stuff was and pretty soon they had a system running where they traded big plastic containers of the alcohol in exchange for food and diesel for their tractor. The tractor wasn't much use for farming the rock-hard ground, but hooked up with a flatbed trailer it was invaluable as a means of transport to and from the nearby villages, where they sold most of the hooch. Of course they consumed large quantities of the stuff themselves. For them it was a sustainable and happy life and it was one that we easily slipped into ourselves.

*

We felt very comfortable at the farm. As a chemist, I think I helped them quite a bit by showing them how they could mix the alcohol with other ingredients to use it as a fuel for stoves and even the tractor. After this they treated us like we were one of the community, so we relaxed into the swing of things. One way or another we ended up drunk most nights and sleeping most of the day. There was a kind of communal hubble-bubble pipe too. I'm not sure what they put in it but it made us very calm. Too calm perhaps. I suppose I was trying to show Sean that I wasn't such a middle-aged square. After all I had been through some pretty wild times when I was young at university, but I was not used to this kind of thing at all, especially given the frame of mind I was in at the time, with my wife having walked out and all that.

So you may be unsurprised to hear that what with all of this merriment, Sean and I somehow managed to lose track of time. I know it seems hard to believe, but we must have been shacked-up there for over a week without realising it, until one day we came to the horrifying realisation that our visas had run out. I had heard stories of tourists being thrown into jail for overstaying their visas back then, so I felt sure the Chinese authorities wouldn't look kindly upon us. Our excuse was hardly one that would induce sympathy.

After a long discussion, Sean and I came to the conclusion that we were better off making do on the money we had left and trying to make it into Laos. This, our farming friends told us, was known as a fairly easy border to cross unseen. Looking back on it now, I can't quite believe I thought this was a wise idea, but then who knows what might have happened if we had turned ourselves in? We might still be there, rotting in jail. And it was a hell of an adventure really, what we did. Thousands of miles we walked, down through rural China, keeping away from main towns and larger roads. We felt like escaped prisoners of war. The longer it went on, the more serious we realised our plight would be if we were caught.

Mostly we slept in woods and thickets during the day and walked by night. We agreed that buses were too much of a risk unless we got picked up casually, like hitchhikers, which the odd bus driver was inclined to do. The ticket offices in bus stations invariably asked to see passports and would religiously check the visas of foreigners before selling them a ticket. It always worried us that drivers might be told to do the same en route.

Sean and I wore worker's clothes and carried hoes or rakes in order to look like peasants. We developed a sixth-sense for the places where we were likely to be checked and those where they would leave us alone. I did send a letter to the university saying I had been delayed through illness. I might have guessed they would never receive it.

We had many adventures along our route to Laos – some strange, even frightening and others downright hilarious. But I particularly remember one night in Anhui Province, near to the town of Tangkou. After more than a week of walking in rain through a rough, muddy region, we reached a village named Qingyang. The people in Anhui province, I remember, were quiet and less inquisitive than in most of the areas we had been through. It was the early hours of the morning and the road was deserted. As we entered the outskirts though, we saw what we discovered to be a small run-down guesthouse on a corner, with a very welcoming rose coloured glow emanating from the foyer. We were really in need of a bed, having slept badly on rocky ground for the last two nights. Sean was still recovering from a bite wound after being attacked by wild dogs when we were washing by a river. We took a careful look in through the window. Someone seemed to be asleep down behind the reception desk. We could see his feet sticking out. Gently Sean knocked on the glass door and a small, bleary-eyed man surfaced to let us in. The dark wooden building was like a rickety old galleon, with dimly lit, narrow gangways and creaky, sloping decks. The whole place was listing over to one side.

Paying only a few Yuan in advance we were shown a small room upstairs, which we accepted gladly. Thankfully no papers were requested.

Next-door to our room, Sean and I took turns in the basic communal shower. It was great to get clean. A bedraggled looking woman in a dressing gown was waiting outside as I came out. I apologised, feeling guilty for keeping her waiting. It was around 3:30am. Perhaps she was getting up early for work, I wondered?

Sean and I got into our hard, narrow beds at around 4am and switched on the portable black and white TV. A film or something might help us sleep, we agreed, and as we were paying for it we thought we might as well make the most of the luxuries.

We must have dropped straight off to sleep, because at around 4:15 we were awoken by a knocking at our door. Both of us sat bolt upright and stared at the door. Our first thought was that the man on the desk might have alerted the authorities, but the knocking seemed too gentle.

"The TV must be disturbing people," I whispered. "It's probably the guy from behind reception."

We remained suspicious and rather scared but there seemed little point in not answering, since there was no window to escape from anyway. After giving it some consideration, Sean got up and unlocked the door. Immediately he did so, a woman in pyjamas pushed her way in and shut the door behind her. Her finger was held tight to her lips.

Sean gasped, at pains to understand what was happening.

"What the hell?" I exclaimed.

Perhaps the woman was trying to escape from someone, I wondered. She switched on the dim room light, seeming to know exactly where the switch was in the dark. Still by the door, Sean backed-up in surprise. Our visitor looked to be around forty years old – fairly plain, with hair wet from the shower. I recognised her from earlier, outside the shower cubicle. A strong floral scent had wafted in with her.

"Masaji? You want masaji? Only fifty Yuan for two peoples."

She began making hand gestures in case we were not yet aware of what she was offering.

"Ehm, this is my son," I replied. "I am the father...Papa. Pleased to meet you."

Sitting up in bed I held out my hand formally, thinking she would get the message, but no. In retrospect, I can see we were at this point the woman's only chance of business for the night, so no wonder she persisted.

Still determined, she tried other gestures. She certainly didn't need language; the gestures were most explicit.

"Sorry, it's kind of you to offer, but I am father – FATHER…Fu Chun! This is my son." I made my own gestures. They did not help. She remained perplexed. Sean was offended at the gesticular insinuation that he was a baby.

"Fify Yuan too much for two?" she asked.

I made a sleeping gesture and tried to help her out of the door.

"Tirty – tirty Yuan!" she said. "Cheaps!"

She was in the doorway now.

"OK, OK, twenty-five!" she conceded.

I pushed again. Reluctantly, and with a little more physical encouragement, she went. Stan was laughing by now and so was I. I locked the door and got back into bed, still a little shaken.

"Don't you think it's a bit dangerous to stay now?" said Sean.

He was right. I sat on my bed and thought about it for a moment.

"If we try to leave now, the guy downstairs will be suspicious," I said. "He'll probably think we're trying to scarper without paying and call the cops. No, I think we're probably better lying low. She's not going to tell anyone is she?"

Reluctantly Sean agreed.

We lay there in the dark, nervous about sleeping and listening for a police car outside, but all seemed quiet. It was a bizarre thing to have happened. Several times as we dropped back off to sleep, we woke each other again with spontaneous laughter in the dark.

*

The following morning as we cautiously left our room, we encountered a small dish outside the door. In it was a card with a phone number, two kisses and the name Doris. Beneath it we found two wrapped mints and a folded piece of paper. Unfolding it I discovered a copy of an official document in Mandarin.

"What does it say?" asked Sean.

"I'm just working it out," I said. "I think it's a certificate of personal cleanliness."

"How sweet!" said Sean. "I'll see if there's a back way out."

My Only Friend

"Oh Amirah, you look like you could do with a drink," said Maria. "Forgive me, I've neglected you all morning, haven't I? So inconsiderate of me I know. But there, at least that's the kitchen floor done now, so... just let me get you a drink my dear and I'll come and sit down for a chat."

Maria returned to the terrace with a jug of water and her newspaper. Placing the water on the small table, she puffed up her cushion and lowered herself into the chair. She sighed. Her back and knees were aching. Cleanliness was her passion but housework tired her easily these days. She did her best to be calm, as the doctor had advised her, but there was always so much to keep her busy. The mid-morning sun shone on her. It should have relaxed her, but she chastised herself again – she'd forgotten her sunhat. Her pale skin was sensitive. It betrayed her Basque origins, her husband had always said. But the effort of returning to the kitchen seemed too much. The newspaper would have to provide adequate shade for now.

"Now what was I doing?" she muttered to herself.

A small, feisty woman, Maria had met her husband in Bilbao as a girl, when his ship docked for emergency repairs. Eduardo, the distinguished Portuguese captain, was much older than her and a confirmed bachelor. Until, that was, he set eyes upon Maria. She had served him in a waterfront restaurant, close to the docks. Many times since, he had told people how her frosty grey-blue eyes and sharp features had captivated him on that day.

"I carried her off," he used to say. "Brought her home like an adventurer returning with treasure."

Maria had ceased reading her newspaper now. She sighed as Eduardo's kind face entered her thoughts. The glint in his eye that had always been there whenever he looked at her. She was drifting into sleep, as she so often did nowadays. Fading images of her life with Eduardo filled her mind.

"It wasn't always wine and roses though, Amirah?" she pointed out.

Relocated to Lisbon after a whirlwind, three-day romance, they had been married quietly in Eduardo's family church. Maria had settled into his large but somewhat austere house in the outer suburbs. She had never belonged there, and she told her husband this. She missed the bustle of a city. So Eduardo, eager to make her happy, had bought the apartment for her in central Lisbon, close to the Basilica Da Estrela. It was a relief, yet somehow she had remained dissatisfied. Of course she was grateful to Eduardo. After all he had rescued her from a life of relative poverty. But Maria hated his long voyages away. She had felt like a prisoner in Lisbon back then. She had never complained of course, but Eduardo knew. He had hoped the birth of Ignacio would be a solace, and on the face of things it was. He was such an angelic little boy and she had doted upon him; dressing him smartly and feeding him treats, like a little prince. Other issues had become secondary after that. Ignacio became her primary focus. And perhaps too much so, she conceded now. Every childhood ailment or grazed knee had brought the world to a stop. "Ah yes Amirah, in the early days you know, I had to have the doctor out at the merest hint of a sneeze."

Maria chuckled to herself. She was not quite asleep. A breeze rustled her newspaper and she folded it into her lap to prevent it from blowing away. Reminiscing had a tendency to leave her sad, but it was almost all she had now so she was not about to give it up. And she still held onto a hope that she might find a solution to her problems with her son. They hadn't always been enemies, after all, she reminded herself. But alas she felt irritable now.

The problems had emerged fairly early. As Ignacio had grown into a young man, so he had begun to distance himself. He became defiant. Despite her husband's assurances, Maria was sure she had not imagined it. She was a simple soul but she was not a fool. And it was more than just intuition. There were things that Ignacio knew were important to her. First of all he had refused to speak Basque with her and had begun to spend more and more time alone in his room. He would find excuses for her not to meet him from school and gave her the wrong dates for sports days or prize-givings. Other parents must have noticed of course. What if they thought she didn't care about her son, she had asked him? But Ignacio had always been a determined boy. He had told her if she turned up he would not compete. It had been so humiliating. Didn't all parents like to share in their children's achievements? Maria sighed. And why had his father not spoken to him about it? It was not as if she hadn't told him often enough.

At a certain age, Maria remembered, Ignacio had begun to behave in a very male way. Just like his father did in fact – that swagger in his walk and the way he listened when another man spoke but seemed almost not to hear anything she said. But when she had pointed that out, the two of them would say that she had imagined it. They became more and more like members of a private club really. She hadn't imagined that either! She had noticed how the two of them always skulked off together when Eduardo was home – finding excuses like they were going to the hardware store to look for a particular kind of wire to make fishing flies, then not coming back until late, smirking with the smell of drink and cigars on them. Oh of course they were men and so why wouldn't they behave like that? But it had upset her. Pride had not allowed her to show it. As always, she had kept her objections to herself. And that was when she had found herself a job, at the laundry. Needless to say her husband had disapproved of her doing menial work. She couldn't deny she had taken some pleasure in telling him that she felt comfortable there among what she described as *her own kind of people.* "Well, I needed friends, didn't I Amirah?"

*

The newspaper was flapping again. It roused Maria momentarily, but she had no desire to get up. She preferred to remain where she was – lost in the past. There was singing coming from the Basilica and it lulled her back to her daydreams.

It was when Eduardo retired that things had really changed. She had thrown herself into looking after him, she could see that now. A new routine had emerged where she had concentrated on meals – the special things Eduardo liked – and on keeping the apartment clean, orderly, the way he liked it. But all this had seemed to irritate Ignacio, she remembered, and her husband had sided with him. She became increasingly irritated by the pair of them, always seeming to be waiting for her to go off to work so they could relax and enjoy themselves. She had never mentioned the smell of cigars on the terrace or the empty brandy bottles in the dustbin store, however much it had irked her. And didn't she deserve some credit for that?

It was natural of course that Ignacio had felt a special bond with his father, and his father with him, given all the time Eduardo had spent away at sea. It was the way of the world – Maria knew that well enough. Of course Eduardo had a special allure for Ignacio when he returned with exotic presents and stories of adventure. All boys loved that kind of thing didn't they? Nonetheless, these were uncomfortable things to think about even now. Painful memories that she had never shared, except with Amirah. It would have seemed selfish. Jealousy is such an unattractive trait, her mother used to say.

It was barely a year into his retirement when Eduardo was taken ill. What began with a bad cold, had progressed to pneumonia. She blamed it on a fishing excursion he took with Ignacio. He should have taken his warm coat as she had told him. She had wanted to nurse him at home and was furious with their doctor for having him taken into hospital. She had fought to keep him at home, but the doctor ignored everything she said. That male arrogance again. She knew her husband better than anyone, so why was her opinion worth so much less? And Ignacio hadn't stood by her either! She had watched him exchanging glances with his father, as if there was some unspoken agreement between them. Something she wasn't to know. It still incensed her now. It would never leave her, the memory of that day. The smell of the baked cod that she had cooked him for lunch; it was his favourite, yet he had hardly eaten a scrap. She remained haunted by the image of Eduardo's drawn, grey face, looking back at her as the ambulance men carried him down the staircase in a wicker chair. The way his glassy, shrunken eyes had seemed to be avoiding hers. Why? Was it her fault – had she not cared for him well enough? His eyes had been closed by the time she arrived at the hospital. She never saw them open again.

Maria sat up. "This is no good, no good at all!" she snapped. "All these negative thoughts, Amirah. Mother of God, I've had enough of it!"

Unfolding her crumpled newspaper, she began turning the pages – shaking them straight out of a sense of irritation with herself. Surely she could find something to distract her from this self-indulgence? But it clung onto her. Especially the issue of Ignacio, her lost son.

Unsurprisingly perhaps, Ignacio had become ever more distant after Eduardo's death. She had hoped that if Eduardo's departure resulted in anything good, it might be that Ignacio would become closer to her. It had seemed possible to her that he would realise how valuable his remaining parent was to him, now he had lost the other, but no. And therefore soon after, the inevitable had happened. Ignacio had found reasons to move. There was more chance of him finding a job if he lived nearer the centre, he told her. She had objected but it was as if he hadn't heard a word she said. He incarcerated himself in a dark basement room on the other side of the city.

"Do you know, it smelled even before he moved in, Amirah. Why anyone would want to live in such a miserable place is beyond me!"

In Maria's mind Ignacio was in the midst of a process of slow decomposition. Rotting away there in all that filth. And he sulked. She could sense him there, sulking even now.

"You know it's almost as if he blames me for his father's death. Yet how could I have done more to care for Eduardo? I devoted myself to him in those last years, you know I did Amirah. And it's not as if I didn't try talking to Ignacio about it – try to mend the bad feelings between us. I tried several times to broach the subject before he moved out, didn't I Amirah? But no, each time he cut me short and just stormed off. What more could a mother do, that's what I'd like to know?"

Reaching for her reading glasses, Maria's attention was drawn by the water in the jug, rippling as another tram juddered away from the tram-stop below.

"Oh for goodness sake, how silly of me Amirah!" she said, "I'd forgotten all about your water."

Maria picked up the jug and began pouring it gently, her thin sinewy arm shaking with its weight.

"There you are dear, I did warm it for you, the way you like it. Some things I do still manage to remember." She watched as the water gently soaked into the soil around Amirah's tangled roots. Amirah seemed relieved. Unfolding the newspaper, Maria smiled at her and began to read aloud.

"Arctic Weather Conditions Approach Southern Europe. Goodness me Amirah, it's only just November and it says the cold front may soon reach the Iberian Peninsula!"

It did seem hard to believe. Stretching out before them from the third-floor terrace, there was still a heat haze hanging over Lisbon. It combined with the smog and dust from the early morning commuter traffic that was still swarming through the old streets below them. Maria had grown used to the noise, but memories of this view in the early days were floating around in her head – a time when the city was less frantic. It had been poorer then, but somehow so much more humane.

There were very few pleasures in Maria's life nowadays. Eduardo was five years in the grave and it seemed clear to her that Ignacio would care little if she were in hers. She had even stopped going to church following a bitter argument she'd had with Father Mateus over Eduardo's funeral. He'd always been so understanding, until then. But it was not all doom and gloom. Not by any means. Now and again she went to play bingo with a couple of the women she used to work with at the laundry, and most Sundays she had a nice walk, taking flowers to her husband's grave. And of course there was Amirah. Ah yes, Amirah was a good companion. Absolutely! It would be no exaggeration to say that without her, the last five years would have been intolerable.

Maria smiled and gazed at Amirah lovingly. They had shared a lot really. Like her, Amirah had been brought to Lisbon by Eduardo after one of his trips. In Amirah's case, from the Far East. Customs restrictions had been looser back then. Maria had warmed to her straight away. If only Eduardo had known how much of a help Amirah was to be to her after he died. Perhaps he had, she wondered. But things with Amirah had not always looked so fortuitous. She had taken time to settle. The thought of it now still troubled her. She had not flourished there. If only they could have asked her what was wrong. It was she who had noticed how much dear Amirah liked being out on the terrace. She seemed to cheer up almost immediately, bless her. Eduardo had thought it was the sun and fresh air, but Maria had been sure it was more about being able to overlook the goings on at the tram station. She understood her. They understood each other.

The sun was shining directly upon Amirah now but she seemed to be enjoying it. She looked radiant. Maria had worried initially about making the terrace Amirah's home. It was large enough, but then Lisbon did suffer from the occasional cold snap. To pacify his wife, Eduardo had fixed up some hooks so that they could hang heavy polythene sheeting if the weather turned cold. He'd made a good job of it, but Maria had still worried about Amirah not being able to see the comings and goings at the tram station. So in the winter she developed a habit of taking the sheeting down in the day and replacing it at night. Nothing was too much trouble.

*

In so many ways, Maria and Amirah's present situation was ideal. It was something Maria constantly needed to remind herself about. She had a tendency towards pessimism, Eduardo had always said. She and Amirah were company for each other after Ignacio left and Amirah had certainly become more relaxed. The truth was, Maria felt, Ignacio had never been kind to Amirah. He had even had the audacity to say she was just a plant. Maria suspected he was jealous of her. Indeed, any mention of Amirah had made him furious. He had, Maria reminded herself, behaved like a volcano about to erupt when she told him she might move Amirah into his room after he moved out. How ridiculous?

"He's so selfish, Amirah" she muttered. "Typical! Not a thought for your welfare, or his mother's for that matter. The ingratitude of the man. And after all I did for him as a child!"

Anger and frustration over Ignacio seemed to constantly dog Maria. All those years of putting him first, and for what, she asked herself, abandonment? And it was not as if she hadn't tried. She had called around to see him several times after he moved – taken one of his favourite almond tarts – but she had not felt welcome there. Besides, Ignacio's reluctance to work, bathe or make any effort to look presentable, assaulted her senses. It was an affront to her tidy disposition. Almost as if he were purposely trying to antagonise her.

"I told him, Amirah, your father would fill heaven with his tears if he saw you like this. But did he listen?"

Hours of sitting on her terrace going over all of this was the reason Maria's resentment had grown. Somehow she knew this. She clutched her head. Her blood pressure was rising again.

"Yes, it's a woman's lot to be taken for granted, Amirah. Husbands, sons; I tell you, they think the woman is there purely to serve them. Now you, you would never be so selfish, I know that. Yes, I've stopped visiting him. Of course I have, I mean what's the point? I'm not wanted there am I? I mean even chance meetings have become unlikely. The way Ignacio likes to live – at the opposite end of the day, playing computer games alone until dawn and then sleeping until evening – it doesn't invite sympathy, does it Amirah? You know I'm ashamed to say it, but he's become a good for nothing slob." Maria rubbed her nose distastefully. "Ach, the disgusting thought of him lying there, festering in his filthy, sweaty bed; growing fatter by the day while I wear my fingers to the bone keeping our floors and surfaces spotless. Mother of Christ, it burns my very soul, Amirah, it really does!"

Finally it was the clatter of the letterbox that roused Maria from her tormented ramblings. Putting down her newspaper, she got up to check what letters had arrived. She sighed. It was actually her birthday today, for all that mattered. Not that she received many cards anymore. She bent down with a groan.

"Bills," she grumbled. "Only bills Amirah." Maria shuffled back to her armchair. "Nobody remembers you when you're old, dear, but at least we have each other, eh? Bless you, Amirah."

*

Lying there in the darkness, Ignacio lit a cigarette. The red glow reflected off the grubby whitewashed walls as he drew hard on it, causing the room to glow. He looked up from his bed at a large mosquito, aware that it had already bitten him. He could kill it, he thought, but then why bother? He watched the engorged insect as it buzzed about and came to rest on a tattered postcard of Benares. Pilgrims bathing by the steps of the Kedar Ghat. He had come across it in an old suitcase the previous day and stuck it to the wall with chewing gum. His father had sent it to him when his ship was in India. Ignacio still remembered the pride he had felt, taking it into school for show-and-tell. At this moment, however, it was causing him intense feelings of discomfort. Clutching his grubby pillow, he buried his face in it. He cursed himself and his situation. His father would never believe it if he saw him living in this place. How had he ended up in this predicament, he asked himself?

But Ignacio knew the answer. Spite. Pure spite. He had been determined to teach his mother a lesson. To show her what happened to a child whose mother always cared more for how things looked – what other people thought – than for the actual welfare of her child. What happened to a child deprived of love when a mother thinks more of a stupid plant than her own child? When she talks to that plant more, and loves it more than her son? His lips tightened with resentment. Nothing he had ever done was good enough for her. Not like his father. His dad had been a friend to him. They'd had such larks together when he came home. Yet his dad had loved her, he couldn't deny that. Adored her. He would never have spoken ill of her in front of his father. Little by little, as Ignacio lay there looking up at the postcard, remembering his childhood and his father's kind voice, he became overwhelmed by an aching sense of regret. His misery deepened.

What would his father think of him for treating his mother this way, he wondered?

Catching a distorted glimpse of himself in the cracked mirror, Ignacio was shocked by what he saw. How pathetic he looked; a grown man whimpering into a dirty pillow. And for what? To spite his mother, for her unbearable obsession with niceness, cleanliness and giving a good impression to others. He had certainly achieved that, but it had given him precious little satisfaction, if he were honest with himself. It was himself he had done the most harm to. He couldn't go on like this, he knew that. He had to find a way to put an end to it, even if it meant putting an end to his life. His miserable life. If only he could sleep. Sleep forever, he wished, yes. He took another sleeping pill and a glug from the glass of stale water. He lay waiting, his eyes wet, but sleep would not come.

*

Ignacio had lost his sense of time. He was sure he had not actually fallen asleep, yet the sounds of rattling keys and car doors slamming had roused him. Sounds of the early morning, as people began leaving for work. These thoughts of life going on in the street outside were a timely distraction from his worries – his thoughts of ending it all. Mercifully though, the tension in his body seemed to have let go at last and he could feel that sick sense of helplessness ebbing away. It was getting light; a time of day he had long become unfamiliar with. Somehow the emerging daylight had brought with it a pale sense of fresh hope.

Ignacio opened his eyes properly. A crack of light had broken through the blanket he left permanently hung at his window. There had never been curtains. His skin tingled as warm blood seemed to have begun flowing around his body. He could feel it – hear it too. His heart pumping. He felt afraid at first but it was an exhilarating kind of fear. What was happening to him, he wondered? Was he having a heart attack? Was this in fact the end he had wished for?

Ignacio sat up and rubbed his eyes. Stretching towards the window he attempted to lift a corner of the blanket to look out. As he did so it fell and in an instant he was bathed in bright sunlight. Shielding his eyes he felt suddenly overcome. A sense of awe. A visitation of sorts. Almost that he might be undergoing preparation for a new start. Gradually it became apparent to him that there was some good left in the world. Perhaps, he told himself, it was not too late to put things right? This was what his father would have wanted him to do.

His fragile optimism growing, Ignacio made a hesitant resolution that when it got fully light, he might begin this new-born day by contacting his mother. The fact that it was her birthday had not escaped his conscience that week no matter how hard he had tried to forget her. Perhaps he might even take her a birthday card? She certainly wouldn't be expecting it. Ignacio sunk back again into his pillow, finally able to relax. Yes, some things were too late to change, he knew that, but with others there was still hope. Over the last three years he had failed to acknowledge his mother's birthday at all. That had been intentional, but this year would be different, he told himself. Reaching up and taking down the old postcard, he reread his father's closing words.

"Treasure your mother, you are everything to her my son."

With a sense of purpose that had long abandoned him, Ignacio got up and began rummaging through his chest of drawers. Eventually he managed to locate the birthday card he had failed to send to his mother three years ago. Moving into the shaft of light from the window, he took a pen and began writing.

Dearest Mama. I have been selfish in neglecting you, I know. Be assured I have always cared about you despite my absence. I have been in a dark place, but from today everything has changed. The light has returned. Happy birthday, your loving son, Ignacio.

He stared at his words for a moment then slid the card into the envelope, taking care not to mark it with greasy thumbprints. Placing it carefully against the framed photograph of his father, he lay back down. Gently his head met the meagre pillow. There was hope now. Yes, she had driven him away with her pampering, but wasn't this out of love for her only child, he asked himself? And to be fair, she had only transferred her love to Amirah *after* he had rejected her. He shuddered again at the thought of his mother's nauseating diatribe with that plant. It had been a destructive downward spiral from then on with wrong on both sides, but there was no point dwelling in the past. It could be mended. He was sure of that now. He just needed to take the first step.

Ignacio's tears ran freely as he lay looking at the ceiling. Desperate for security he pulled the covers around him, but his tears were no longer tears of despair. Over the years he had come to detest his mother's fussing and her fastidious housekeeping, yet now he would give anything to be lying in his bed at home, snuggling down into those fresh, crisply ironed sheets. He sighed deeply and as he did so he seemed to let go of any last vestiges of anger he had felt towards her.

*

As Maria awoke, she sensed it was late afternoon. The aroma of spit-roasted piri-piri chicken was being carried up on a draught from the street below, accompanied by the sound of school children leaving the tram station. The sun had moved around to the side of the building and the terrace was now shaded and chilly. Disorientated for a moment, she sat there gathering her thoughts. Ignacio had been in her mind, hadn't he? But no, she was worried about Amirah. That was it. Goodness yes, there was a sharpness in the autumn air!

All of a sudden she remembered the weather forecast.

"Don't worry Amirah dear," she said, momentarily panicked and struggling from her chair, "I'll soon have you warm and cosy again."

Maria bent down to lift the plastic sheeting. Her joints had gone stiff. Strangely, when she heard her front doorbell ring it was with a sense of having heard it ringing in her sleep. It seemed to repeat around and around inside her head.

"Oh for goodness sake, who can this be now?" she grumbled.

Nervously, she lifted the latch on her front door. Standing before her was Valentina, one of her friends from the laundry. She seemed breathless and red faced.

"Oh thank goodness, Maria!" she said, holding out her arms. "How are you darling? I tried phoning earlier but... whew... no answer. I half expected to find you out." She hesitated to catch her breath. "What is it dear, you look startled?"

"No, no, I'm pleased to see you, as you can see," laughed Maria uncomfortably. She clasped her hand to her chest. "A little dizzy, but all in one piece nonetheless. I was probably asleep on the terrace, I think. Come in, come in, those dreadful stairs have worn you out."

"Look, I won't keep you if you don't mind," said Valentina. "I don't want to dirty your clean floor, and anyway I need to get back to make Enrique his tea. I just called to say that Asun and I wondered if you'd like to come to bingo tonight. It's a bonanza night, with a ten-thousand Euro cash prize for the big game!"

Valentina emphasised the amount. Money was a big thing to her. Maria could see she had already taken the opportunity of the change in the weather to show off her fur coat.

"Oh dear, Valentina, that's so kind of you, but you know how I hate to rush," protested Maria. "I mean, look at the time. I'm really not sure what to say."

"Don't be silly," said Valentina, "at our age we need all the nights out we can get. There'll be no bingo at our funerals! Now look, I've arranged to meet Asun outside the old ballrooms at seven, so no more nonsense about time, we'll see you there, okay?"

Reluctantly Maria agreed. She stood listening to Valentina's heels clicking down the stairs. Perhaps this was in aid of her birthday, she considered. But Valentina had certainly not mentioned it. Anyhow there was no time for this now. Quickly removing her floral pinafore and putting on her coat, Maria picked-up her handbag and set off downstairs to the small shopping arcade, hoping they might be able to fit her in at the salon. She could always eat something later, she supposed.

*

As it transpired, the hairdressers had suffered a cancellation, so they were able to offer Maria a wash and set if she could sit down immediately. It panicked her a little, but then it would save her going back up the three flights of stairs. And she had lipstick in her bag.

"Are you going out somewhere then?" asked the girl, testing the water temperature on her wrist.

"It's my birthday. I'm going to bingo with my friends, but..." She looked again at her watch. "Oh dear, it's all a bit of a rush you see."

"Not to worry, dear," said the girl, "we'll fast-track you."

Maria was about to say that was kind of her, but she hesitated. She was not sure she liked the idea of being fast-tracked. The girl was also chewing gum, and that was a habit Maria couldn't abide. Worse still, the girl's top was too short and Maria noticed she had a silver pin through her bellybutton. It didn't bode well. She was glad when an older lady took over after the washing. It also transpired that this older lady was the sister of someone Maria had worked with at the laundry.

"It's a small world. I don't think I've seen Carla for... oh it must be two or three years," said Maria.

"No, well she's moved to Oporto to live with her son and daughter-in-law. He makes a fuss of her. Didn't like the idea of her living on her own after her husband died."

The woman walked over to collect the lotion.

Maria blanched. She was going off this one too, she thought as she studied herself in the mirror. What Eduardo had called her laughter lines had become misery lines. Not a day had passed after his retirement when he hadn't told her how beautiful she was. Evening light from the street glinted on a tear as it formed in one eye and Maria had to remove her arm from under the gown to wipe it away before the woman noticed.

*

Ignacio rang the bell one more time in case his mother was asleep, but there was no response. Pushing the card carefully through the letterbox, he clomped down the stairs and shuffled along the precinct to where his moped was parked. The smell of the spit-roasting chicken seemed to catch hold of him as he passed, and drag him back.

"Half a chicken, crispy, with chips, wrapped, and I'll take an extra leg to eat now," he mumbled.

The man regarded Ignacio, pensively.

"You used to live along the road with your mother, didn't you?"

"What? Oh, I did, yes. I've moved now."

"Hmm, that's right yes, Maria isn't it? Lovely old lady your mother. Always has a smile and a kind word for everyone."

"Well yes, I suppose she does," muttered Ignacio. A

pang of guilt had struck him. "Yes she's well liked, that's true."

Ignacio took a bite of chicken as he left. He had been about to make a sarcastic comment about how mothers fuss so unbearably but he had stopped himself just in time. What an asshole-son he would have appeared to be, he thought. If he really wanted to put things right, perhaps he should take more notice of how others perceived her. He could start by telling her what the chicken man had said in fact. What a pity she'd been out.

*

Maria was busy paying the hairdresser as Ignacio walked past, licking the grease from his fingers. Her attention was fixed upon the fact that she had little money left in her purse and would need more to go to bingo. The bank was in the opposite direction and to make matters worse, no trams ran that way. She could get a taxi of course, but this would leave her with less money for bingo. Despite being fast-tracked she was still pressed for time. On balance it seemed sensible to walk straight to the bank. She thanked Carla's sister and rushed out, failing to recognise her son riding past. She stepped off the curb, coughing amid the cloud of two-stroke exhaust smoke Ignacio had left behind.

Rounding the final corner Maria was relieved to see no queue ahead of her at the cash machine. She quickened her pace in case someone else arrived. It seemed to her a cruel trick to arrive and find the screen displaying a message saying it was out of order.

"Maria Fernandez, your luck tonight is not good, not good at all," she chided herself. "You should have stayed at home with Amirah as your instinct told you to!"

The wind seemed to whip-up at that moment to torment her further. She wished she had put on a warmer coat. Getting her hair done always put her in a good mood, but this had now been well and truly spoilt; probably by the thoughtlessness of some young bank clerk or children pushing things into the slot, she told herself. With a growing sense of persecution, Maria flagged down a taxi and climbed in.

"The bingo hall at the old ballrooms please," she said. "I'm in a bit of a hurry but I wonder if you could stop quickly for me on the way – at the cash machine by the war memorial?"

Racing through backstreet shortcuts the driver eventually screeched to a halt by the machine.

"Such a helpful young man," Maria said to herself, entering her PIN. "And what a shame they're not all like that!"

"Off to bingo for the evening then are you love?" asked the driver as they set off again.

"Yes, it's my birthday," she smiled, checking her hair in the mirror. "I'm meeting a couple of friends."

Glancing into the mirror, the driver returned her smile as he pulled up in front of the ballroom steps. The sense of kindness she already felt about him was verified by his refusing of her tip.

"You spend it on the bingo, dear," he said with a wink. "I've a feeling you're going to be lucky tonight, you mark my words."

The taxi sped off again, leaving Maria momentarily happy. But images of her no-good son kept forcing their way into her mind. Images of him climbing out of his dirty bed in his pants and vest; making coffee in the same cup he had drunk soup from the day before. She muttered something about him always forgetting her birthday, but changed her face quickly back to a smile when she saw her two friends.

"You seemed miles away then, Maria," said Asuncion. "How are you darling?"

She was fatter than ever, Maria thought, but still trying to squeeze into the same clothes – clothes that had always been too young for her anyway.

The three women embraced and headed inside, not noticing the taxi driver waving as he swept by with a new passenger. They were late and the wind was icy-cold now. Paying for their cards they just managed to get to their seats as the big game was about to start. The hum of an eager crowd hushed as the caller cleared his throat, tapped the microphone and introduced himself.

"Can everybody hear me?" he chanted cheerfully.

"Well it's the big one folks. If you haven't been to the toilet it's too late now. Yes we've got a nice turnout. We're going to have a wild night tonight!"

Like the converted ballroom, the ageing caller, with his dinner suit, bow-tie, slicked-back hair and waxed moustache, seemed like a relic from a grander past.

"Get on with it then!" someone shouted. "If I'm here too long my husband will run off with his fancy woman."

The crowd howled with laughter. They were ready for a good time. But Maria felt out of place; still convinced she should have stayed at home.

The first calls passed with Maria drifting in and out of thoughts about other things. Valentina had to point out a few numbers she had missed. Maria stared up at the flaking, ornate ceilings, picturing the evenings she had spent here dancing with Eduardo. She shivered as the scent of his cigar smoke returned to her. How times had changed. She didn't even like bingo. Anyway, Eduardo used to say it was common. Valentina and Asun, being seasoned experts, played four cards a session. Maria always stuck to one. Had they really not remembered it was her birthday, she wondered? Neither of them had mentioned it. And Ignacio – how could that lazy good-for-nothing son again neglect to even send her a card or telephone her? She was his only living relative. Was Amirah the only one who cared about her now?

"Amirah!" Maria shrieked, startling the people

around her. "I forgot to cover the terrace. Oh my poor Amirah I've left you in the cold!"

"What on Earth's the matter with you Maria?" hissed Valentina. "Are you trying to get us barred from here?"

As serious players, the shushing from around the hall was mortifying to Valentina and Asun. They would think twice before inviting her again. With a face of numb panic, Maria leaned across to whisper an explanation into Valentina's ear. Meanwhile Valentina tried to continue playing her cards.

"It's too cold to leave her, Valentina, she's old and frail!"

There was nothing else for it, she would have to go home immediately and put up the sheeting. Maria began gathering her things.

"Telephone your son, for goodness sake!" said Asun leaning across, a sense of urgency in her voice. "He can ride over on his moped and put up the sheeting. You can't possibly leave now woman, you nearly have a full house!"

"For the love of the Madonna be quiet!" insisted a woman in a headscarf in front.

Maria peered down at her card. It was true. Only one more number to get. A seven – her lucky number.

Aware that Maria was about to drive those around them over the edge, Valentina nonetheless fumbled in her bag with her free hand and passed over her mobile phone. She was beyond caring about the objections of other players.

"Ignacio, it's me, your mother, I'm calling from Valentina's mobile phone. Ignacio I..."

"Mama, I came over earlier to..." began Ignacio, but Maria cut in on him.

"Look Ignacio listen, I am at bingo. Can you hear me? I need you to go to my apartment, Ignacio. I wouldn't ask you but it's a matter of life and death!"

Several people around them row began expressing their irritation and disbelief by huffing and muttering. Ignacio listened patiently.

"Ignacio, I need you to put up the plastic sheeting, or Amirah will freeze to death. I don't know what else..."

"Okay Mama, okay, I understand," said Ignacio. "I'll get straight over there now. It'll only take me ten minutes, now stop worrying. I promise I'll do it. I'm on my way out of the door, now please, go back to your bingo. And Mama..."

Fumbling with the buttons, Maria switched off the phone and passed it back to Valentina.

"Well?" whispered Valentina.

"It's... it's okay," said Maria, her voice distant and perturbed. "He promised he'd be there in ten minutes!"

Maria remained stunned. Had she totally misjudged Ignacio, she wondered?

"Have you quite finished?" asked the enraged headscarf woman in front.

"Yes I have thank you," smiled Maria. "You can relax, I'll be quiet now. It's my birthday you know."

Already furious, the woman's face swelled like a huge inflamed boil waiting to burst.

"Gone to heaven, number seven," said the caller, holding up the ball.

Maria remained silent.

"Maria!" gasped Asun. "Maria… number seven!"

Maria put up her hand but said nothing. She had been told once too many times to be quiet.

"Bingo!" shouted Valentina. "Bingo!"

A rumble of voices began, and then built like distant thunder around the huge auditorium. Hundreds of wide eyes turned to see who had called. Their eyes fell upon Maria, who was now on her feet with her arm in the air, but still silent. Some of the previous complainants close by looked far from pleased for her.

"It's that stupid bitch with the mobile phone," she heard someone say.

One of the comperes minced up the aisle and

confirmed that Maria had indeed won the evening's cash bonanza prize with only a single card.

"It's a bloody disgrace, that's what it is!" spat the headscarf woman. "An outrage. She should be disqualified, her!"

*

Across the street, in the bar of the faded Palacio hotel, where she and Eduardo had spent their wedding night, Maria insisted she should get home to check on Amirah. But her friends were determined to celebrate her success, since she had now also divulged that it was her birthday.

"Well that's settled it then," said Valentina. "Ignacio has taken care of Amirah, now allow us to take care of you. Waiter! We'd like three glasses of sparkling wine...no, what am I saying, make that a bottle."

It was nearly midnight when Valentina's husband dropped Maria home. She hadn't had such a good evening since Eduardo passed away, she told them. Fumbling and feeling unusually inebriated, she managed to unlock her front door. She was just about to pick up a pink envelope from the mat, when someone called her name from behind.

"Mrs Fernandez?"

The policewoman asked if she might come inside. After picking up the mail and placing it on the hall table, she sat down with Maria on the sofa. It seemed that

Ignacio had been involved in an accident on his moped. He had skidded on an icy tram rail and gone under a taxi. The policewoman didn't need to tell her that Ignacio was dead. Maria knew that already. Kindly she made Maria a hot drink, gave her a sedative and settled her into bed. The policewoman had not wanted to leave, but Maria had insisted she would be happier on her own.

"One of my colleagues will call by in the morning, dear," she said.

She could see Maria was in no fit state to deal with the formalities of identification. She needed rest.

*

Maria lay in a half-sleep for quite some time, muttering to herself. She had taken a further sleeping pill not long after the policewoman left. Images drifted in and out of her confused mind. Flashing blue lights and people crowded around in a dark, icy street. "Gone to heaven number seven," kept echoing in her head. The taxi driver looking at her in his mirror: "I've a feeling you're going to be lucky tonight, dear, you mark my words." Her husband dead, and now her only son, killed on his way home after doing her a good turn...

Maria's breathing stopped abruptly. But for her blinking eyelids, an observer might have thought her heart had stopped.

Was he on his way home, she asked herself, or had the accident happened on his way there? Maria sat upright in her bed, her clarity returning. Staggering to the kitchen she grappled with the terrace door then flung it open. She was furious with herself. Why hadn't she come straight home? Why hadn't she checked when she got back? She stood at the open door.

"Amirah?" she called pathetically. But she could see it was too late. The sections of polythene sheeting were still hanging loosely at one end where she had left them and Amirah was covered with a white dusting of frost. Maria staggered forward and then buckled at the waist. Unused to alcohol, she began to hallucinate – washed in and out on a tide of delirium.

"Oh my Amirah, what have I done to you, my precious?"

She stroked Amirah's delicate leaves. They were stiff, and broke off at her touch. Tears streamed down her wrinkled face and she slumped into the armchair, crushing her glasses and the newspaper she had left there that afternoon.

"Oh please Amirah, don't leave me all alone," whimpered Maria, sobbing into her hands.

*

After calling by several times that morning and getting no answer, the police finally broke down Maria's front door. From a vantage point across the street, they had seen her on the terrace, slumped in an armchair in her nightdress. Responding over-zealously to a new police health and safety directive, the men put on their white hooded coveralls before entering the apartment.

Her skin had become translucent and her eyes, though partly open, were cloudy and lifeless when they got to her.

The sergeant held Maria's wrist then looked up at his younger colleague, shaking his head. It was too late. She was already dead. Running his hand gently over her lifeless face he closed her eyes. It was not the first time he had needed to perform this duty. It gave him some kind of satisfaction. He had often wondered if he shouldn't have become a priest as his mother had wanted.

As Maria's arm dropped to her side her fingers opened, releasing the crushed green frond she had been clutching in her hand. It fell to the floor unnoticed. Then, almost as if it were not a coincidence, the bright morning sun appeared through a hole in the clouds. Rays of bright golden sunlight were cast down directly onto the sergeant in his white coveralls like a scene in a religious painting. Dazzled, the old woman looked up.

"Am I dead?" she whispered, in a voice barely audible.

The two policemen stood there gazing at her open mouthed for a moment. It didn't seem possible. The sergeant bent down and lifted her frozen body in his arms, carrying her through to the bedroom.

"Call an ambulance," he muttered to his colleague, "and be bloody quick about it!"

But the old woman held up her bony hand, signalling

for him to wait. She was alive and trying to say something, but she was unable to get it out.

"What is it, dear," said the sergeant. "What are you trying to say?"

Maria studied them, gazing at their white glowing forms with an increasing sense of wonder.

Placing her on her bed, the two men came close to her, irritated by her inability to communicate yet concerned about possible accusations of negligence on their part if she were to expire. She was too weak to speak. But her eyes were open wide now, as if she might be afraid of them. Either that or an overwhelming desire to wreak some kind of vengeance upon them. Watching her nervously it seemed to the two men that some great power was welling up inside her. They stepped back slightly in anticipation, although of what they were still not sure. Then, all at once, a desperate choking sound erupted. It was a blood chilling experience for the two men. Slowly, in an eerie, croaking voice, the old woman began to speak.

"I want her... to come... with me."

Maria's voice was still weak, but her determination was remarkable. She gulped for air as the two men recoiled in horror.

"I won't go... I won't... not without her!"

She was pointing towards the terrace. The two men turned and looked outside through the bedroom window, but they saw nobody.

"Idiots!" she growled. "Damned fools! Amirah... I want Amirah with me when I go."

Maria looked very angry. Her eyes burned and it made the two men fear for their lives.

"We're...ah.... We're not...sure...who...you...mean!" said the younger policeman. He spoke slowly, methodically and loudly, as he had learned to do with the elderly. It seemed to infuriate her more. Both men were petrified and thoroughly confused.

The old woman became more exasperated, clutching her fingers into small bony fists. Then her face began to shake. How could she make them understand? She moved her thin lips again, but no sound came out. Nervously the two men leaned in closer to her. Then with one final almighty effort the words spilled out:

"You're the bloody angels, you work it out!"

Burned On Him

"I know you're only trying to help, Pet, but it's no use. Every bloody relationship I've ever had has been the same. And I've tried – believe me I've tried. I don't want it to be that way. I've worked at it – learning my lesson each time, determined to go for a different kind of man – but it always ends up the same way. Aggression. Aggression fired by alcohol, and always so wilfully destructive. Like I deserve it or something. It's become so unbelievably predictable. I think they're different, you know. Each time I'm sure they are, and then slowly it appears, like some kind of malevolent spirit that's been let out of a bottle."

"Hmm," said Petula, examining her nails. She'd had them done last Friday but they were still looking perfect. She knew how much that annoyed her sister. Fran was a little clumsy really. She had famously knocked the top tier off her wedding cake in the middle of their uncle's speech. Thank God their father had not been there. In fact now Petula came to think about it, he would probably have roared with cruel laughter, delighting in the misfortune of others – even that of his own daughters. She had accused Fran of sharing that same trait, and maintained this was a prime example of what her therapist called projection.

"You won't thank me for saying so, Fran," said Petula, holding her hand up to the light, "but my therapist always says to beware of what you see as repetitive bad luck. It's not really bad luck, he says. It's a pattern, and one you can't blame on outside forces."

"Meaning?" Fran was irritated.

"Well, meaning we all find it hard to believe sweetie. I'm the same. I don't want to believe that I'm responsible for my own failures. Far more comfortable to blame the other person, or on bad luck, bad timing or whatever, but the truth is if it keeps happening – I mean however different you think the guy is – then it has to come from you, doesn't it? Fortunately for me I've had the benefit of therapy. And I'm not going to say it because I know how it annoys you, but... well you know what I think."

"Yes," snapped Fran, "and you think you know what I think too! So, leaving that particularly irritating point aside, I'm supposed to be purposely choosing guys with a tendency towards aggression and alcohol dependency – that's what you're saying is it?"

"I'm not saying it sweetie. My therapist said it. It

does seem to have a ring of truth about it though, you have to admit. Why else would it keep happening, mm? It's like we subconsciously look for guys who have those traits, however well hidden, and then we somehow work at bringing those traits out. Crazy! We don't realise we're doing it and it always comes as a shock when it happens, but we're the ones who look for it and, yes, we're the ones who bring it out. Or that's the theory anyway."

"Yes, I like the way you say we," snapped Fran. "Look at you. You've never had a problem with men in your life. Relationships I mean. Take Keith. You set your heart on Keith almost as soon as you met him and he's never been a problem. Eats out of your hand, for God's sake. I hardly think it's a universal problem."

"Oh if only that were true," muttered Petula.

"What do you mean by that?" said Fran.

Petula was not looking at her sister. Her focus seemed to be somewhere beyond the kitchen window, out across the marshes towards the power station. She lifted the shot glass to her lips and snapped her head back. It was a movement that was uncomfortably familiar to Fran. The grappa throbbed in Petula's chest as it went down. She rarely drank. Neither of them did, due to the legacy. It was no understatement to say that their father's alcoholism had wrecked the family. They and their mother bore the physical scars of his violence. The mental scars were only just becoming fully apparent, but they were worse. Far worse.

Petula sighed and ran her fingers through her hair, scoring her scalp with her perfect red nails. She had not always had those nails. For years she had bitten them to the quick. Gnawed at them until her fingers had looked deformed.

"My relationship with Keith is not all it seems, sweetie. Never has been."

Fran hated the way she called her sweetie. They were twins. Petula may have been born ten minutes earlier but it hardly gave her the right to behave like she was the oldest. Controlling behaviour, that's what that was, Fran told herself.

Petula was pouring herself more grappa. It had been intended as a present for Keith. Fran had brought it back from her recent holiday in Italy along with an olivewood breadboard for her sister. Fortunately Keith wouldn't miss it. Poor Keith never expected presents in any case. She should have known better than to introduce alcohol when Petula was around, but she had thought she was over all that. Naïve? Or perhaps subconsciously it had been a test, she wondered. Was she that unkind? They could share the breadboard, Fran told herself.

"How do you mean, not all it seems?" asked Fran, unable to resist discovering more.

Petula was not looking at her. She had turned to look out of the window again. She seemed angry. It was difficult for Fran to see from where she was sitting, but there seemed to be tears in her sister's eyes. It seemed she was not going to answer. That was like their father again. The way he used to throw something into the conversation, like dropping a silent bomb – like nerve gas – and then sit back and watch it wreak havoc. She should ignore it. But that was it, one couldn't. It crept about, invisible and silent, looking for a way into your mind until finally it found one. Devastating.

Fran considered what might have been in her sister's mind, running through various possibilities as she poured herself more tea. Keith seemed so accommodating with her – with everyone really. It was not as if he was one of those macho guys, determined to keep women in their place – he was kind. He supported Pet – spoiled her even. It was hard to believe he had a dark side. Take the way he had got up early this morning to cook them all breakfast before he went to play golf. It was a case in point. So what could Pet be alluding to, Fran wondered?

"Too much like Dad," muttered Petula, all of a sudden. "More than you'd think, sweetie. More than you'd think."

"But he seems so..." began Fran, puzzled.

"Yes, don't they all, sweetie," replied Petula, turning. Her eye make-up had run. "But I mean it. Just like him! It's uncanny. The way he knows how to say something at just the right moment to absolutely put the knife into me. Only with him it's worse. He seems so placid that nobody else realises he's doing it. It makes me want to... well you know... to explode. I'm surprised you don't see it?"

Fran was silent now, trying to get her head around what her sister had said. Had she really not picked up on what Keith was like? She was usually so observant where people were concerned. But quiet people, they were often like that weren't they, secretly provoking, devious, manipulative? They could be anyway. But Keith... surely not? No, this was a classic example of Petula's particular brand of spitefulness, she could see that.

A crunch of gravel on the drive caused the two women to look outside towards the gate. It was Keith's car. Seeing them at the window he waved as he pulled around in front of the greenhouse.

"Thoughtful as ever, you see," said Petula, acidly. "Making sure he leaves the garage clear for Mum and Bernard. Keeping them on his side. Oh Petula dear, Keith is such a treasure – so considerate. Huh, such a manipulator more like!"

Fran studied her as she took a tea-towel and wiped her eyes at the kitchen sink. Perhaps they'd had a row, she wondered?

"How are we all here then?" asked Keith cheerfully, entering the kitchen by the back door. Petula did not answer, she had gone back to staring at the horizon.

"Fine thanks Keith," said Fran. "Mum and Bernard went to shop for dinner tonight. Still not back yet. How was the golf?"

"Oh, so so really. The guys I was playing are retired. You know, out every day. But it's not about the winning, I try to remind myself."

"Hmph, good luck with that then," muttered Petula sarcastically, pouring herself more grappa.

Keith looked over at her, his cheerful face falling. He seemed nervous all of a sudden.

"Did you manage to get to the hairdressers, darling?"

"Well I'm glad you can tell the difference," hissed Petula. "I didn't as a matter of fact. I've been too busy talking to Fran...about men."

Chilled by her sister's words, Fran turned to look at Keith. His eyes were already fixed on the glass of grappa before Fran lifted it to her mouth. She swallowed the contents in one gulp. Watching his wife from behind now, Keith remained frozen; a hand slightly raised as if he might have been going to do something with it. To ask her to stop, perhaps, or place his hand gently on her shoulder to soothe her. But whatever his first intention, something had made him think better of it.

Fran waited, saying nothing, hoping that her sister might suddenly soften and welcome her husband back, but no. Rigid on her kitchen stool, Petula remained propped up on one arm against the breakfast bar, her eyes fixed on that power station in the distance. It was as if she knew something was going to happen to it. That it was suddenly going to explode or something.

In the end it was the sound of another car sweeping across the gravel drive that awakened the three of them from their frozen state.

"Oh how nice," muttered Petula. "Now we can play happy families. Let the charade begin!"

Opening one of the cupboards under the kitchen worktop, Petula leaned down and placed what was left of the bottle of grappa inside, next to the cleaning materials.

"Wouldn't want to bloody well upset anyone," she mumbled. She was beginning to sound a little incoherent now.

"I was just saying to Bernard, so lovely to come home to one's family, rather than an empty house. How are you all my darlings? How did the golf game go, Keith?"

"He lost, mummy," said Petula. "But apparently winning is not Keith's thing. How was shopping?"

"Oh the usual really dear. No green beans, no mange tout, but we got you the muesli you like."

"The muesli was for Keith, mother," snapped Petula, clawing at her scalp again, Keith likes muesli, I hate it. I don't know how many times I have to say that. One could be forgiven for thinking that after thirty eight years of motherhood a mother might know what her daughter likes for breakfast, don't you think?"

"Oh dear, someone's got out of the wrong side of bed this morning," said their mother. "I think a cup of tea might be in order."

Whilst explosive atmospheres and family arguments had been a daily fact of life when their father was around, things had always been calm since he left. The girls had gone through a period of seeing him once or twice a year during their teenage years, but after a while they had both decided to cut all links with him. It was nothing to do with Bernard arriving on the scene, despite what their mother liked to believe. Their father was poison to them. They had both agreed that they were better off without him. But not seeing him had failed to prevent his continuing to damage them. They had burned themselves on him ever since, their mother once said. There was a genetic legacy, according to Petula's therapist, not to mention what a child learns growing up in such family circumstances.

Fran looked around to find her stepfather. How was he managing the situation, she wondered? Bernard was the strong, silent type. Kind. The polar opposite of her father. He thought before he acted. And he was totally devoted to her mother. In fact, wasn't Bernard the kind of man she herself should be looking for rather than those self-satisfied public school types she usually went for. A younger version maybe? Bernard was looking concerned. Meeting Fran's eyes he smiled.

"I'll get the shopping before that ice-cream thaws, said Bernard calmly. I wonder if you could give me a hand Keith?"

A look of palpable relief on his face, Keith excused himself and slipped past his mother-in-law to exit with Bernard via the back door.

"What's wrong with you these days, Petula sweetheart?" asked her mother. "You don't seem yourself."

Petula sighed and began drumming her perfect nails on the kitchen worktop. Somehow the sound was deafening. Her mascara was running again.

"Have you been to Doctor Patten? There's a woman doctor there now you know."

"Yes, interesting isn't it," hissed Petula, "how you assume the problem is with me mother, rather than anyone else. Menopause, that will be it I suppose? Women's trouble. God I'm beginning to see now how your subtle provocative remarks must have had their effect on Dad!"

"Petula, that is so hurtful!" replied her mother. "I never provoked him, you must know that?"

Fran was finding the conversation between her mother and her sister somewhat surreal but at that moment something occurred that she couldn't ever remember happening in their house before. Petula broke wind. There was no hiding it. In fact it had seemed intentional.

"Petula!" exclaimed her mother in horror.

Petula said nothing, she just reached over and opened her handbag. Her face grew steely as Fran and her mother looked on and her lips thinned as if she were deciding what to do next. Then out of the handbag she took a packet of cigarettes and a plastic lighter. Shaking, Petula took out a cigarette, placed it in her mouth and lit it. The other two women were aghast. It was unthinkable.

"But Petula darling, you don't smoke," said her mother, "you've never smoked!"

Petula drew hard on the cigarette, causing it to crackle as it burned. A cloud seemed to fill the kitchen as she tilted her head back and exhaled sensuously.

"And how would you know that, mother?" snapped Petula. "How the fuck would you know?"

In the tightly stretched tension of that moment, Petula's mother had lost the colour from her face. Unsteady, she grabbed onto the back of one of the breakfast bar chairs. She had learned to expect personal attacks from her ex-husband but she had never experienced aggression from her daughters, not even verbal aggression. It was unbearable to her. Devastating. Her bottom lip quivered as she tried to speak.

"Bernard... Bernard?"

Fran was not looking at her mother. Something else had distracted her. Juxtaposed with the rising tension in the kitchen she was faced with a silent backdrop of Bernard and Keith outside in the drive. They had unloaded the shopping bags but were now in animated conversation. Keith's face appeared very serious. Bernard, meanwhile, seemed to be explaining something to him. Fingers were being pointed. Behaviour that seemed out of character in of them.

*

"Hello Francis, I am detective Anderson. Please call me Lauren, if you'd like to. Now, I want you to remain calm, Francis. You're in the hospital, do you understand? You've been injured but you're going to be okay. Now, I need you to try to tell me what happened at your parents' house."

Fran's head felt numb. How long had she been asleep, she wondered? The woman's words seemed to resonate around the room as if she was in some kind of hollow tank. She looked down at herself and at the gown she was wearing. How did they manage to make them so unattractive, she thought to herself?

"Do you remember being at your parents' house, Francis?"

Fran closed her eyes. She didn't want to think about it, yet closing her eyes seemed to make it seem more real.

"Are they all dead?" she murmured.

The detective hesitated for a few moments, as if perhaps she hadn't heard anything. But she was trying to decide. Trying to remember the correct procedure in such cases.

"Except for your brother in law," said the detective, "yes I'm afraid they are. And I need your help, Francis. In order to begin to understand what happened."

"Fran," she replied. "My name's Fran. Only my father called me Francis. He's in the garage " She sighed as if finally realising she was safe. "I locked him in there."

Fran raised her right hand and examined the bandages.

"I need to phone and tell my team," said the detective, getting up from the chair.

"Be... be careful!" called Fran, as the detective opened the door.

The detective stopped abruptly and turned.

"He's got a golf club," said Fran. "I think it's a nine-iron."

A Minor Distraction

Sighing, he allowed the book to drop onto the table. He couldn't remember when he had last read a book that really held his attention. Pulling the curtain slightly open he looked out onto the platform. Why was the train waiting so long, he wondered, it was in the middle of nowhere?

For some reason the station was crowded with people. They were squeezed shoulder-to-shoulder onto the short platform, struggling with their bundles and emaciated livestock. Flies buzzed around them in the heat. Christ, Africa was intolerable!

"Do you people even know how crap your lives are?" he muttered. "Spending your morning frying on a station, knee deep in cow shit with flies crawling into your mouths?"

He sat up and drew the curtains. The book was boring. Maybe he could find more to interest him outside. He surveyed the faces of the people on the platform. Weathered, dusty black faces, some scarred from childhood diseases. People with with clouded and missing eyes. Missing limbs too. Hunch-backed, toothless old women with stick-thin buckled legs. It was a freaks' menagerie.

In the shade of the station he saw a long snake of people leading to a ticket window – a remarkably civilised queue in such a primitive scene. His attention was drawn to a woman in that queue who seemed agitated. The woman kept standing on tiptoe trying to see something beyond the crowd. Following the direction of her gaze he noticed a young girl, waiting nervously at the edge of the platform. The girl was strikingly beautiful – no wonder the woman was nervous about leaving her there, he thought to himself. This was more interesting to him. Carefully rising to his feet, he pulled down the window of the carriage door. The heat overwhelmed him immediately and he winced. The girl was close by. Hearing the screech of the window opening, she turned towards him.

"My God, those eyes!" he whispered to himself. "Hmm, lets try a little challenge shall we?"

He glanced back over at the woman in the ticket queue. She looked more unsettled, like a hen who had sensed her chick was in danger – a predator close by. His eager stare returned to the girl, who smiled at him then lowered her eyes quickly.

"Excuse me!" he called out. The girl looked up. "I

want to talk to you for a moment. Do you speak English?"

She nodded and took a few cautious steps forward as he beckoned to her.

"Outrageous!" he murmured, watching the graceful movement of her young body. "Come closer dear, so I can talk to you. Don't be afraid."

The girl looked over her shoulder at the woman, presumably her mother. The mother hen had lost sight of her chick and now seemed quite upset.

"Caroline!" she called, Caroline!"

He smirked. "Caroline," he said, with a satisfied smile. "Now then Caroline, listen to me. There's not much time, the train is about to leave. I am a professor. I'm from America. I am very rich and I want to help you. I will be frank with you; I want you to get into my carriage. I will take you back to America with me, away from all this misery and filth, but you must get onto the train quickly, Caroline. Do you understand?"

"But why do you do that sir?" said the girl. "Why you want to help me?"

He glanced over at the ticket queue. The mother hen was at the front of the queue now and was fumbling with her handbag. This challenge was going to go right to the wire, he told himself. He would need to act quickly if he was to succeed.

"Look at these people, Caroline. Diseased, broken, no hope, no future; do you think your mother wants that for you? I don't think you belong here, do you? You know you don't! Get into my carriage, Caroline; this is your last – your only chance of escape."

"Caroline!" called the mother hen again. Her cry sounded desperate.

With a clunk the train wheels moved and in a flash the carriage door was open. Seconds later Caroline found herself inside, heart pounding like a gazelle cornered by a panther. She held her breath. How had she got there, she wondered? Had she really stepped into the carriage by herself?

"Well done Caroline, your life will be happy now, and you'll be safe," he said, closing the door.

He studied her, frozen for a moment as the train began gathering speed.

"My God if you're not the most beautiful girl I've ever seen," he said under his breath.

Fear took hold of her then as she looked into his eyes.

"W…why do you take me go to America with you sir?" she stammered, grasping the door handle.

"Caroline, Caroline, calm down my dear," he said sweetly.

"Why, tell me why, sir?" she demanded.

He was shocked at her sudden forthright demonstration of anger.

"Okay, I'll tell you why," he said, trying to buy time. But doubts were creeping in. Already he was beginning to wonder how he would explain the girl to his wife.

"Now Caroline, you know when you see a beautiful thing in a shop window. He hesitated. "Let's say like a diamond tiara – and you want it so much that you absolutely must have it? That's how I felt when I saw you on that platform."

He smiled – pleased with his explanation.

"I don't know what is a tiara, sir," said the girl. "But I know what is diamonds. My mother say my father died in the diamond mine to make white man rich." She was crying now. "My mother tell about temptation. About the trap. Yes sir, and now I am in the trap – God help me. Yes, you will harm me I think!"

"Caroline calm down, you're a fool if you think I want to harm you," he said.

But she did not calm down. Caroline was in a state of growing panic. Reaching up, she grasped the door handle. Realising he was losing his hold over her, the man held onto the door tightly.

"I want to help you, you silly bitch," he snapped. "What would you prefer; to stay here in this filth and disease with these no-hopers, or to come with me and live like a princess, hmm?"

He chuckled to himself. He felt sure he had hit the spot now. The challenge was not lost yet. Not by a long chalk.

"I don't want to be princess," she growled. "I am sick; I only want to be well."

At this she turned the handle of the door. The train was now moving at speed and had long passed the end of the platform. The man was fixated upon what the girl had just told him. He stepped away from her instinctively, covering his mouth. No longer restrained, the carriage door suddenly flew open. The girl was there, and then she was not. There was a tearing sound as her dress caught on the handle for a moment, then a scream and she was gone, beneath the train.

*

Placing her change in her handbag the mother hen pushed her way through the crowd onto the platform. Her chick was not where she had left her. Surely she would not have boarded the train without her? She looked along the platform.

"Caroline," she called, "Caroline where are you?"

A group of old men pointed along the line towards the departed train. The woman looked down the line. Other people were looking along the line too. A porter was running towards a bundle by the rails. Then he stopped. They saw him raise his arms and clasp his head.

Meanwhile, the man on the train carefully closed the

door and slid the window up. Sitting back on his unmade bed, he pulled a white handkerchief from inside his shirt cuff and began meticulously wiping his hands. Moments later he swung around, startled by the sound of his compartment door opening.

"Darling you look pale," said a tall woman. "You really should have come to breakfast. Somehow they managed to get smoked salmon this morning. I mean, earlier you said you were looking forward to breakfast, and then you changed your mind. You really are the most indecisive man. I wonder that you ever managed to propose to me at all."

The woman sat down opposite him. She smelled of floral soap. He went to replace the handkerchief in his sleeve but hesitated and dropped it into the waste bin with an expression of distaste.

"Just... a minor distraction," he said, examining his fingernails. "I am just so bored with Africa, Lillykins. I really think we should get a boat home from Cape Town. I miss the cats."

Removing a silver case from his jacket pocket, the man selected a cigarette, took a lighter from the table and lit it. The woman watched him – the way he did everything so slowly and fastidiously. It was becoming infuriating to her.

"And what about me," she said. "I suppose I don't matter?"

"Of course you matter, Lillykins. That's why I bought

you a honeymoon present, silly."

He fished into his inner jacket pocket and handed her a small envelope. She received it with a suspicious smile, opening it cautiously as if it might contain a dangerous insect.

"Diamonds?" she said, tipping three large uncut stones into the palm of her hand. She gazed at them, wide-eyed. "John, you shouldn't have... They say people die for these you know."

"And so they do my sweet. In fact I don't doubt that this is the greater part of their allure. But enough of that; I have an appetite suddenly. Come, lay yourself beside me."

The River Witch

Wild camping has its disadvantages. Having pitched his tent by a riverbank in the dark, Finn had accepted that he would sleep only fitfully. It had been hard to survey the area properly last night and he knew he would be on edge; constantly expecting to be disturbed by a gamekeeper out looking for poachers, or in the early hours by someone walking their dog. It was fortunate then that heavy rain in the night had made passers-by less likely. The incessant sound of the rain had finally helped him to drop-off and left him sleeping until the early morning sun reached his tent. He lay there now in half sleep, listening to the sound of the fast flowing water; the river swollen by the unseasonal rainfall. The sounds of nature were all about him; an enthusiastic Song Thrush; a duck drying its wings; a bumblebee buzzing around the tent. Finn reached out and groped blindly for the tent zip. Finally accepting the need to open his eyes, he squinted out at the river and hooked back the door. A slight breeze circulated around the inside of the tent and cooled his bare chest. His eyes were now open, but he was still not entirely awake. Taking a swig from his water bottle, he propped himself on his elbow, lazily watching the river. Swallows swooped low, following the winding shape of the river. Dragonflies hovered; a beautiful naked girl swam by; a Bullfinch... "What, a naked girl?" muttered Finn, sitting up with a start.

By the time Finn had registered that he was not in the midst of a dream, the girl had gone – swept along downstream by the fast moving water. Maybe she had fallen in, he asked himself? No, she had been too calm. Out of his sleeping-bag now, Finn clumsily began pulling on the damp cycling shorts he had left to air on his crossbar. Determined to delay no longer, he dived in. Freezing! He glided under the rushing water for a moment then swam hard crawl for a minute or two in response to the cold. Then he stopped, captivated by the beauty of it all. Regretting the disturbance he had caused with his pounding strokes, he floated along silently downstream, trying to take everything in. River weeds stroked his chilled under-body as he passed, warming him slightly. He marvelled at the reflection of the overhanging trees on the water, the sun glinting through and the variegated green hues on the glassy surface. Hearing a large bird take flight from a branch above him, he rolled over onto his back to see a heron heading off downriver. As he floated on rapidly, he watched it all going past, absorbed in the sounds, the aromas, the vivid colours and the activity. The scent of mint filled his nostrils for a moment or two; musty cow parsley;

comfrey and newly mown hay. A duck's nest appeared in an uprising of rushes; a clutch of blue-green eggs shining like perfectly polished turquoise stones, but no naked girl. No girl of any description.

He stared up at the brightening sky. Just then a lonely cuckoo called from somewhere in the wood and a small wisp of cloud passed slowly overhead. He felt almost mesmerised, as if he had been transported to another world, where everything was new and unravaged by humans.

Suddenly Finn's head bumped into something; a large log. Awoken from his pastoral reverie, he bobbed about for a moment, before turning over to see where he was. He had been caught by the bank at a sharp bend in the river and was now aware of a rushing sound. He stood up, straining to hear where it was coming from.

"Weir!" a voice said. "Be careful. Lucky you hit the bank."

Finn whipped around to where the voice had come from. Dazzled by the sun he only managed to discern the outline of a figure towering above him on the bank. He shielded his eyes with his hand. A tall girl was standing on the bank above him, that much he could make out – although with the sun still behind her he could not see her clearly. Then bending forward, she wrung the river water from her long hair. As he suspected, she was naked.

"Hi, I saw you swim past further upstream," he said

nonchalantly. "You may have noticed my tent by the bank."

"Tent?" She hesitated. "Do you make a habit of following women when they're out for their morning swim?"

"That depends," he said cheekily.

"I see. Depends on what exactly?"

Finn was stuck for an answer. He hadn't expected a response. Being rather a young man he was nervous. She seemed rather abrupt and he did not feel comfortable having this kind of conversation with a naked girl on a riverbank.

"Look, I'm a bit cold in here," he said. "Do you mind if I get out?"

"Should I mind?" she asked.

"Well... no you shouldn't. Or rather, there's no need to."

"Well that's a relief!" she said sarcastically.

Finn attempted to climb out of the river, intent on doing so with some style.

"Bugger!" he said to himself, slipping back down the bank.

After several more attempts he managed to clamber up. He looked down at himself in despair. He was covered in mud. Better than her having had to help him out though, he thought.

Having moved around to where he could see her properly, Finn realised that the girl was laughing at him. He was also surprised to see, that but for her head her body was entirely hairless and that now he was up at her level, she was in fact rather small. She did not seem at all shy of her nudity. Confident, would be an understatement he thought. Brazen might, however, be going too far. Maintaining his silence Finn wondered about who she might be. Maybe she owns this bit of land? This was not at all what he had hoped for. He thought a girl swimming in the river early in the morning might be more carefree – a little less serious, perhaps? This one was fascinating, but she was positively intimidating at the same time.

She was not really a girl either, now he thought about it – more of a woman. Having given the situation some consideration, he decided it might be better to bring the conversation to a polite close by rounding things off with an explanation. Then he would get on his way.

"Look, I'm genuinely sorry for disturbing you," he said. "There I was lying half awake in my tent, looking out at the river, enchanted by all the swooping and hovering... those watery sounds and the dappled light of the morning sun glinting through the trees. Me, alone, day-dreaming about beautiful fish beneath the surface of the water preparing to leap for insects, and then you slipped through the picture."

"You sound like a poet," she said. "Are you a poet?"

Finn laughed. "No I'm not a poet – just a nature lover; especially of rivers, really."

"Well you should be a poet," said the woman sardonically. "What you said then was beautiful. I can feel those things, I can even be some of those things, but I can't put them into words like you can. No I think you have a talent for it."

Finn was not sure how to take her comments. They might have been sarcasm, he thought. They had been delivered in a rather matter of fact manner. Finn looked at her face trying to determine whether she was humouring him. She stood still, the sun catching beads of water running down her body. Finn also remained still, watching her. She didn't seem to mind. Her skin was pale, almost transparent with visible veins and blood vessels beneath the waxy surface. Her breasts were small, quite muscular really, and there was river-weed in her hair. Overall she seemed nice, he thought, but she had come across as rather ill-tempered at first – almost aggressive one might say.

"Mm, such a beautiful picture," she murmured gently – as if to contradict him. "I hope I didn't spoil it – swimming through your picture like that?"

"Oh no," said Finn, "not at all. You were an essential part of it actually. You were like some graceful creature gliding by. I hardly registered that you were there at first. You blended into the scene like you belonged there, and with the river flowing so fast you were there and then you were gone. It took me a moment to realise it wasn't a dream actually."

Finn looked into her eyes, aware that he may have gone too far and frightened her. Maybe he had been too intimate? Why couldn't he just be cool? She was looking away now. Scanning the surrounding woods and fields of hay. She looked distant. A little melancholy perhaps. He felt unkind for having wanted to abandon her.

"I'm Sorry," he said again. "I just meant to say that if it did disturb me, it was only in a positive sense. Clearly this is your special place. It's probably your land and I have no right to expect to have the river or the morning to myself."

"Why do you keep apologising?" said the woman.

Finn hesitated. "Well, as I say, I wondered if this land belongs to you."

The woman laughed. "No! No it doesn't. But the river does – or rather I belong to the river."

"That's beautiful," murmured Finn, quietly. It was reassuring to hear her laugh. But the woman had sat down on a fallen tree and was now leaning pensively on one raised knee. She seemed to have become serious again. Finn felt worried that his decision to hang around might be the cause.

"Er, I need to get back to take down my tent," he said. "People will be out walking now and I don't have permission to camp here."

"We could swim back upstream together, if you're strong enough," she said, her spirits lifting again slightly. "It would be easier than trying to walk along the bank."

Finn doubted that. However, such an offer, proposed in the form of a dare, made it hard for him to refuse. He moved to climb down the bank, but remembering his manners, stopped and held out a hand to help her down. Seeing her cold reaction he cursed himself for patronising her. Finn stood there awkwardly, hoping he could retrieve the situation. He just didn't seem to be able to get anything right with this woman – except for the poetry perhaps.

There was a splash. She had taken a shallow dive into the river. He looked on anxiously, convinced she must have hit the bottom, but the sun was reflecting on the surface of the water making it impossible to see her. Had she hit her head, he asked himself? He slid down the bank quickly and into the river.

It was an arc of water that blinded him. Raising his arm to his eyes, Finn recovered and saw her there, laughing. Another arc of water cut across him then she turned and dived under again. Accepting the challenge, Finn dived down after her, kicking hard against the strong current, pulling his arms through the thick water. He could see her pale body illuminated by the sun as it made its way shimmering through the weed. He saw her look back and smile before performing an exquisite swirling turn and continuing upstream. This woman was incredible. What a swimmer, he thought! She moved through the water effortlessly, often without even using her arms. Studying her movements, he saw how she kept both legs together and bent at the waist, then kicked both legs together to propel herself forwards. It was as if she were a dolphin. So effective was her technique in fact, that he had no chance of keeping up with her. Racing to the surface for air he regained his breath, panting, and stood in mid-river looking upstream.

"Where in the world are you?" he called, laughing.

Suddenly there she was ahead of him, exiting the surface of the water dramatically as if she had come from somewhere way down in the depths. The water ran off her face. Opening her eyes she smiled and looked at him playfully.

"What's your name?" he called.

"Why do you need to know?" she replied with a girlish laugh.

"I want to know who you are," he insisted. "Where you're from."

"I'm a fugitive from the deep," she said.

"What a romantic!" Finn thought. But he wanted more than that. He had to know her better. He wanted something to hold onto. He sensed she might disappear at any moment.

The woman smiled, then turned and dived under again.

"Bloody hell!" he murmured, "I'll never keep up with her."

Finn tried swimming on the surface, looking out for her below, but he was getting nowhere. Where was she?

Afraid that this time she might not return he dived under and began swimming through the white-water shallows, looking around for her. He was beginning to despair when all of a sudden he saw a movement ahead of him down deeper, among the darker weeds. It was her, but she seemed far below – too far. The river couldn't be that deep, surely? He swam down deeper, clearing the pressure in his ears.

Passing down through the bright green weed, Finn noticed how the current was weaker down there, making it easier to swim upstream. It felt almost unnatural – too easy. The water was also less murky and he began to see quite clearly. Amid caves and strange aquatic plant-life, Sticklebacks and shoals of Rainbow Trout glinted momentarily in the small amount of sunlight that managed to penetrate this far down. He could still see her below, but she was going ever deeper now and it seemed too dangerous to follow her. Sensing his apprehensiveness she turned to look at him. She smiled, signalling for him to follow her. But at that moment he became aware of how long he had gone without air and despite not having felt the need of it before it pained him.

Panicked and kicking hard, Finn rose quickly up through the rippling undertow towards the sunlight and eventually emerged, gasping for air. His head was spinning; partly from lack of oxygen but also from the incredible sights he had seen below. It had seemed so real. He looked around. The woman had not resurfaced. Surely, he asked himself, nobody could stay under for that long? Fear touched him at that moment like a cold hand from the dark and he shivered. Maybe he should get out and walk along the bank, he told himself. He might be able to see her from up there. But looking at the bank he could see this section was too overgrown with brambles to walk along in bare feet. He began to swim hard, but as before he made no progress.

Finally, accepting there was no alternative, Finn dived down again. Struck by the silence, he fought his way back down through the oily weeds, but this time he went deeper, all the time looking for the woman. Yet despite his desire to find her, Finn found himself distracted by the strange underwater landscape; the rocks and caverns, long flowing plants wavering in the current with tiny silvery bubbles of air caught on their leaves. He touched the bubbles gently, watching them quiver and rise to the surface like shimmering capsules of mercury. It was all very surreal – beautiful and yet somehow sinister.

Then a moment later, without warning, she appeared from between the leaves ahead of him. Finn swam hard, his heart racing, through some long spiny leaves, between the rocks and into what seemed to be a sandy clearing. Deftly her body arched and she raced away from him, turning for a moment to see if he was behind her. Catching a glimpse of her face, however, he realised immediately it was not her. She was younger. The girl looked in fear for her life. Finn drew back. Fear gripped him too and he realised he needed air again. The girl darted quickly in amongst some dense purple weeds. He couldn't turn back now, he thought. He must follow her.

Grappling his way through the weeds, his chest aching, Finn kicked hard again, propelling himself forward. Gradually the weed thinned as it gave way to the mouth of a large cavern and he saw her – the young one. No two... three of them! They seemed nervous and determined to get away from him. He must surface now. His lungs felt like they might burst. One of the girls stopped and looked back, holding out a hand towards him. No, it was her!

Finn's heart raced as he swam desperately towards her, but the younger two women gripped her by the shoulders and pulled her away. Unable to escape, she looked back at him sadly. Then in a moment she turned and swam away, lost in the darkness of the cavern.

*

Bursting through the surface of the water Finn filled his lungs and found himself able to stand again, but he was dizzy and unsteady on his feet. Wading further into the shallows by the bank to get out, his feet sinking into the soft mud, he looked up and was surprised to see his tent and bicycle. He surveyed the scene. It was familiar, yet it still felt like a fantasy world – a place of dreams. Almost like somewhere frozen in his distant past. Nothing had physically changed, he could see that, but his view of it had changed – his sense of it. He felt almost like an intruder now. Gently he felt his knees bend and the water rise up his chest as he sank back into the shimmering liquid. Pausing for a moment as he threaded his way back down through the long slender weeds, Finn looked up at what he was leaving behind him. The sun was flashing reflected shapes and verdant colours as the trees moved in the breeze. A leaf landed on the surface of the water and he waited a moment to see it carried off downstream. Moved by the beauty of it all, he turned reluctantly away and dived deeper, down through the murky depths towards the bottom where it cleared again.

More graceful now, Finn curved his body just as she had and swept between the boulders, deposited there by the great flood. On he swam through the purple weeds and back into the dark mouth of the cavern where he had last seen her. This time the fear that had previously gripped him and the pain in his lungs were absent. In its place had grown a delightful sense of belonging.

Riding the current, Finn swept through into the darkness where he knew she would be waiting for him and calm descended on him like a warm blanket. There close by, her voice whispered to him out of the darkness.

"You're safe now my darling."

Finn's body was relaxed now and a feeling of radiant

bliss entered him. It was as if he was undergoing a transformation, yet he knew neither what from, nor what to.

His conscious mind having been awoken, Finn stiffened. Something was not right. Was this really what he wanted, he asked himself? He was submitting to something – allowing himself to be taken over somehow. Mournfully he thought about the view up at the surface. The leaf falling on the water and being carried away downstream. The scene and sounds that had met him when he awoke. He didn't want to leave all that – to exchange it for this darkness and silence. Was that the deal, he wondered? She hadn't told him. Surely he had a right to know what to expect?

All at once Finn became aware of his chest beginning to ache again. He clasped his head. It felt as if it was being crushed by some enormous pressure. His strength was leaving him. He could feel it ebbing away as he held his eyes tightly closed.

"Don't leave me now," her voice said, echoing in his head. "Stay with me, please."

Out of the dark, her delicate fingers touched his. Then, like a warm rush, relief came to him. The pain and anxiousness had gone again and he felt no need to struggle. Time was meaningless now. It was over. Water rushed in his ears. A blinding light shone from somewhere above him as he opened his eyes and he saw the bright surface of the water racing towards him. Bursting through the silvery skin, he felt the sun warm him as he turned and splashed down on his back. There he floated, remembering how to breathe.

"There's pike in there mate," said a voice. "Whoppers! River Witches they used to call 'em."

Finn looked up to see an elderly man walking past with a black Labrador.

"Some lads have gone in there and never been seen again, I tell yer. They'll bite the nuts off yer, you mark my words!"

The sound of the man chuckling to himself petered out as he disappeared through the cow parsley. Finn clambered out. He looked down at himself as the water ran off him.

"Hmm, a lucky escape."

Traffic

I had been warned not to expect things to run even half-efficiently in Africa, but I was sort of prepared for it. Every time I go on trips to developing countries it's something; they can't find my booking when I arrive at the hotel; there's no car to meet me at the airport, or if there is the driver makes a long detour to a shanty village to drop off a chicken to his sister. Take your pick from a long list. I've learned not to let these things get to me, to be more philosophical, but some things are more challenging than others. On one trip I checked into a smart hotel and went to my room, only to discover that the toilet was missing – a ragged hole left in the floor. I reported it to reception and they told me the last occupant must have stolen it. Hard to get your head around really.

My interest in primitive art developed into a business a number of years ago, following which I focussed mainly on the Far East. I must have made nearly a hundred trips there. My first trip to Africa came about five or six years later. Although I have learned to accept that life works differently in different cultures and that there is little we can do to change it, nothing anyone had told me about Africa could have prepared me for the reality of what I was to experience there.

During that first visit to Africa, the inconveniences I suffered proved far-reaching. Life-changing in fact. It seemed straightforward enough making the arrangements. I flew to the Cameroon to meet an art dealer. I suppose I was quite excited about the trip, now I come to think about it. Problems first began to arise on the way in from the airport when a woman stepped out in front of my taxi. I remember we were passing through a rather chaotic roadside market on the outskirts of Douala. I'd noticed her running along at the side of the road, slightly ahead of us, and I was just asking myself how on earth she was managing to run over sharp stones and pieces of debris with bare feet, when all of a sudden without warning she darted out into the road in front of us. The picture of her face as she turned to look at us, is forever burned into my memory. It was a look of absolute horror. Not at the fact that she was about to be run down, I later realised, but over whatever or whoever she was running from.

The woman seemed to just stand there transfixed and allow the car to hit her. The sound as she hit the bonnet of the taxi was sickening and I found myself clasping my hands to my ears. The driver got out quite casually it seemed to me, as though these things happened to him every day. I saw him walk around to the front of the car and look under it, where the woman was now lying. A crowd of people, some carrying bags full of brightly coloured vegetables, gathered around. The driver got back into the car and reversed slightly, nearly running down several onlookers in the process.

"Very sorry for the inconvenience sir," the driver said.

"Shouldn't someone call for an ambulance?" I asked numbly.

"No no sir," said the driver, "she has gone to the Almighty. Somebody has gone to look for her family so she can be taken to her house. We must maybe wait for long time sir. I am sorry for your delay."

Bizarrely he seemed eager to reassure me that he had switched off the meter. Did he think my mind would be on that rather than the death of this poor woman, I asked myself?

Moments later a policewoman arrived on the scene. Pushing her way through the crowd she looked at the victim and then came around to the window to speak with me.

"Your passport sir," she said to me curtly, holding out her hand.

I fumbled in my shoulder bag and eventually found it. The woman flicked through it roughly then put it in her shirt pocket. Seeing my concern she leaned forward to explain.

"This is a serious incident sir and I must ask you to come to the police station to answer questions."

I was perturbed at this change of tack. Up until that point it had seemed anything but a serious incident to the people who had witnessed it. There was the driver, sitting down casually at a roadside stall, smoking and having a cold drink – making the most of the time, in fact. The policewoman went over to speak with him, after which he reluctantly shuffled over to remove my luggage from his boot. The policewoman motioned me towards the police car parked nearby, while the taxi driver brought along my suitcase. Having placed the case in the boot, the driver stood there awkwardly.

"He is waiting to be paid sir," said the policewoman.

Somewhat dumbfounded, I opened my wallet and handed the driver a large note. I generally carry quite a lot of money with me on these trips, since I often need ready cash to purchase work from individual artists or smaller dealers. The policewoman seemed agitated at seeing the large wad of cash and hurried the driver away. I suppose it was careless of me, but in my defence, I was still in shock.

Down at the station they asked me to explain what had happened, which I did. It all seemed pretty straightforward. They listened, made a few notes and nodded positively. After this they kept me waiting for some time while they typed a report on an old typewriter. All a matter of third-world bureaucracy, I told myself. Finally the policewoman came and presented me with three copies, pointing out the places to sign. It was in French. My spoken French is okay, but I have difficulty reading it. In any case, I could see that the statement was incorrect.

"Not necessary to read sir. It is a formality. Just sign," said the policewoman smiling.

"It's in French," I said. "I can't sign a statement written in French," I said. "Anyway, I need to have a lawyer present before I sign anything."

The assembled representatives of third world petty-bureaucracy and law enforcement looked at each other and sighed.

"It is Sunday sir," said a man in plain clothes. "If you need a lawyer you must wait until tomorrow and we must keep you here in the station prison. Because you are a witness, do you see? Do you understand?"

I looked him hard in the eye as if to tell him I certainly did understand. I was not naïve.

"I have to say, it would be better for you to sign sir," the man said, smiling. "Then you can change it later if you like. I'm sure you have important business. We don't want to inconvenience you."

Things were beginning to worry me by now. Judging by the state of the toilet, I certainly didn't want to spend a night in their cells.

"I would appreciate it if you would please call the British High Commission," I said.

"No, no, there is no point sir," said the woman. "You are forgetting, it is Sunday so they are also closed until tomorrow."

She waved the papers at me and held out the pen.

"I'm sorry but I insist you let me phone the British High Commission," I said more assertively. "There will be an emergency 24hr number; please get it for me now."

The wait was excruciating, but within an hour a man had arrived from the British High Commission along with a lawyer. I apologised for disturbing them on a Sunday, but they passed it off as nothing serious. I explained the circumstances in detail while they listened. It turned out that the dead woman was a refugee. Can you imagine my horror, when they told me that the police were accusing me of being involved in trafficking refugees as sex slaves? According to them, I fitted the description of one of their chief suspects. The statement they had prepared for me said that the injured woman had been in the car with me and had jumped out in order to escape. I was astounded. The policewoman and her colleagues laughed at my reaction and pointed at me accusingly.

"Do not try to treat us as fools sir," the policewoman said. "We know the face of a guilty man. You are a trafficker sir. When you arrived here to the station I saw it. We all saw it. You had the eyes of the wolf when he is trapped!" The other police officers nodded and mumbled in accord.

Eventually the lawyer asked to be allowed to speak with me in private. This rather shifty man – somewhat unkempt for a man of the law – quietly persuaded me that it was a wise idea to pay the police some money, since the taxi driver had now disappeared and was not able to corroborate my story. Of naiveté I may sometimes be guilty, but a fool I am not. Give me credit for the fact, however, that I was extremely tired and eager to be out of there. I was in Africa after all and I knew this was the way things were done in these parts. So yes, I handed over my cash. No receipt was offered and I was simply advised to be more careful in future. A French émigré at my hotel reassured me later that this was a common story and simply a means for the police to boost their meagre incomes. I didn't know if this should make me feel better or worse. I remember thinking after talking to the émigré, that I would have been happier to give the money to the family of the dead woman. She seemed to have been forgotten in all of this.

In fact I did try to find the woman's family the following day, but nobody seemed to know anything about the accident. I felt bad, but I consoled myself with the fact that I had at least tried to put things right.

*

Further inconveniences awaited me the day after the taxi incident. I had arranged to meet with a Mr Keita –

an art dealer who was going to show me the work of a particularly interesting group of local painters. He had sent me photographs and I felt there would be a good market for this kind of material in Europe. But as soon as I met him, I knew I didn't trust him. When I was younger I was open-minded about people, but I am afraid that I have since learned to be more suspicious. Call it prejudice if you like, but I trust my instincts. I have a sense of what a person is like as soon as they walk into a room. Even if later events indicate otherwise, a lifetime of experience has taught me that my first instinct is nearly always right.

So as I say, I distrusted this man Keita from the outset. His prospects with me were not helped by the fact that when he introduced me to the artists, they were all shapely young women who he openly fondled in my presence. He even suggested to me that one of them would be happy to "look after my needs" during my stay. When I declined, he flashed his white teeth and added that she could bring a younger sister, or brother if that was my preference.

This was most distasteful to me but also inconvenient, since it distracted me from the matter of the work – some of which was really quite interesting. I was particularly taken by a beautiful selection of sculptures that one of the younger women was working on in a disused chicken coop at the back of the building. Nothing, however, would have possessed me to do business with this man after witnessing his unsavoury behaviour. I looked at my watch and made an excuse about needing to meet someone in town. Leaving quickly, I said I might return later, now that I knew where to find him.

"Enjoy your meeting in town my friend," he said, standing self-importantly in his doorway. "I hope she can give you what you are looking for!" And he laughed a disgusting laugh. He knew what white men were here for, he said.

*

Leaving my hotel the next morning after a most unsatisfactory breakfast, I walked along the main avenue underneath the palms. The sun was already scorching the pavements and I began to wish I had brought my umbrella. Seeing an empty bench in the shade, I stopped and sat down to read my English newspaper. It was a newspaper I had picked up on the plane and already two days old, but I didn't mind that. It enabled me to escape the irritations of Africa for a moment.

Halfway through an engaging article about a man who had discovered after years of happily married life that his wife was a ruthless terrorist, I was disturbed by the voice of a young woman.

"Hello, you are Mr Lawrence I think? I'm Lily – I met you at the studio. I'm the sculptor."

Disarmed by this unexpected encounter, I hesitated. I recognised her immediately of course, but I wished to reserve judgement for a moment while I allowed my instincts to decide on how to proceed. Unlike her employer, this young woman seemed trustworthy. I should point out that she was also undeniably beautiful, although this I feel sure was not my reason for inviting her to sit down. Contrary to the suppositions of her boss, I was not here for that.

I looked about, half expecting to see the unsavoury Keita lurking in some doorway, but of him there was no sign. Lily seemed interesting and I really had thought highly of her work. I had made a solemn pledge to myself after meeting Keita never to do business with him, but if she were free to do business with me independently – well that would be an entirely different matter.

"I actually came out to look for a cafe to have some decent coffee," I said, once the usual pleasantries were out of the way. "I'm afraid the breakfast at my hotel was not all I'd hoped for. I wonder if you'd like to join me?"

Lilly looked surprised and rather embarrassed at my suggestion. Not knowing the customs of the country well, it was quite possible that I had offended her and I immediately took steps to deal with her discomfort.

"I was rather hoping I might discuss your sculpture with you, that's all," I explained.

I assume this removed her doubts about my motives, as she then agreed to my invitation.

"I don't know this area well," she said, getting up from the bench, "but I believe there is a very nice French cafe further along the avenue and there is usually a cool breeze from the sea. For that reason I'm afraid we'll be lucky if we get a table."

I marvelled at her excellent English and told her so.

"Nuns are good teachers," she said, grinning.

Although Lily had said she did not know the area well, several of the waiters smiled and seemed to acknowledge her as we arrived. Two of the waiters hurriedly prepared a table in the shade for us, in a prime position overlooking the waterfront. Having at first said she would only have a glass of water, Lily then agreed to join me in a light breakfast of real espresso coffee, croissants and freshly squeezed orange juice.

While we ate Lily talked about her sculpture. At the same time I was interested in hearing about her background and her day-to-day life. I perhaps appeared rather inquisitive in this area, but I was eager to learn more about life in Africa generally.

Reluctantly at first, Lily told me the story of her childhood and that of her mother. Born into poverty like her mother before her, it seemed Lily was the illegitimate mixed-race child of a serving woman – her mother. Lily's mother, it seemed, was made pregnant by her employer's son. Her employer – a wealthy French aristocrat – had apparently sent his amorous son away and threatened to have Lily's mother killed if she breathed a word to anyone. Later the man's wife, a kind hearted woman, periodically sent Lily's mother money to have Lily educated in a convent school. This was where she had learned French and English and where her artistic abilities were nurtured. It helped in her getting a job at a Paris art gallery. In obvious discomfort, Lilly explained how the gallery owner had promised to exhibit her sculpture in the gallery, but that after refusing his advances, she had lost her job.

With no work visa and hearing that her mother was ill, Lily had returned home to Douala. Since then and with little money, she had been nursing her mother back to health. And it was during this time that her mother had disclosed to her the identity of her father. Lily had tried to contact the woman – her paternal grandmother – who had paid for her schooling, but was told that the family had returned to France some time before, leaving no address. Needy young female artists and opportunistic men are drawn to each other, especially in places like Africa. When Lily met Mr Keita he praised her portfolio of sculpture, telling her he could make her rich. Still young and naïve, she had grasped the opportunity of work, hoping it might pay well enough to get her mother some proper medical treatment.

"I don't know why I'm telling you all this," said Lily. "My mother always says I should keep it to myself."

Lily seemed upset. Having met her employer I could already guess the rest of the story. She hung her head in shame as she tried to hint to me what life was like now, trying hard every day to fend off the man's lascivious attentions. Always having to make excuses for why she was unable to go to dinner with his clients. She had stretched things to the limit with him, she explained.

Initially he had probably accepted her behaviour as that of an inexperienced well-bred woman, educated in a strict catholic school, but his patience had begun to wear thin with her now and he was now pressing for some return on his investment.

The idea of this sensitive, talented young woman being roughly handled by that vile man, made me shudder. Watching her trying to fight back the tears as she told me the story was agonising and I ended my breakfast resolved to do something about it.

I had hoped Lily might be available to show me around Douala, but she needed to attend to her mother, she said. What her mother needed though, I realised, was professional care. I had turned the matter over in my mind as we were speaking. I felt sure that it would involve relatively small amounts of money – especially for a man in my position.

"Lily," I said, "before you go there is something I would like to ask you to do for me. I want you to find out how much it would cost for your mother to have the treatment she needs. I mean precisely how much. Could you do that?"

Lily clasped both hands to her mouth. I had expected her to perhaps be embarrassed by my offer of help – I was a virtual stranger after all – but not this. Her face was a picture of complete horror.

"Oh my goodness!" she gasped, "I didn't tell you about my life in the hope that you would give me money. I never dreamed of it. My mother would be furious with me." Lily seemed almost on the verge of tears.

"Lily," I said, "I make my own mind up about whom I help. I am quite a wealthy man, widowed and with no children. I should be allowed to help you and your mother if I want to – if it makes me happy to. I don't think for a moment that you told me for those reasons. It was I who was so inquisitive."

Climbing into the taxi, Lily hesitated, then took my hand. It seemed at first it was a polite handshake but she did not let go. This was not a situation either of us felt comfortable with.

"Mr Lawrence, would you like to come and meet my mother?" asked Lily hesitantly.

Clearly she was worried that their poor living conditions might be a shock to me.

"Call me David, please," I said, "I won't this time if you don't mind, but I would love to call round tomorrow if that were possible. Maybe I could look at your sculpture portfolio at the same time?"

*

Walking back to my hotel, I thought about what had occurred since meeting Lily that morning on the bench. Do we ever do anything completely altruistically, I wondered? I had asked myself this question many times before. There did not, on the face of it, seem much for me to gain from offering this help. Her sculpture was good and this might benefit me as a minor art dealer, but perhaps no more than other work I could find here. I knew others would say I was attracted to her, but I was in my fifties after all and she could not have been more than twenty-five. No, I knew the truth was that I needed to feel I had done some good in the world, for someone deserving. If that meant that I was spending my money for personal gain, some kind of redemption, then so be it.

I thanked the doorman at my hotel, asking myself that same question about altruism as I handed him a large tip. I hated analysing my behaviour. I liked to behave naturally. Yet wasn't that what Lily's boss did? Couldn't he excuse his behaviour in the same way? I pondered the subject uncomfortably as I waited for the lift. No, the big difference between him and I, it seemed to me, was that he didn't care who he harmed in doing what came naturally. Surely we were nothing alike?

*

I slept restlessly that night. It was unbearably humid and yet an environmental conscience prevented me from using my air-conditioning. I say this, knowing that in truth it was the thought of Lily and her fragility that kept me awake – her tragic vulnerability to the desires of men and the corruption of the world.

Finally I gave up on sleep. I took a shower and went down for an early breakfast, this time sticking to tea and toast. I needed to make preparations for my visit to

Lily's house at twelve. I knew I might need more money so I would visit the bank first. After that I would call into the French patisserie and buy something to take to the house, perhaps some flowers as well for Lily's mother.

Lily waved to me from the window as my taxi pulled up in front of her house. Several neighbours came out into their small front yards to see who the well-dressed white man was; a man who seemed to be going to Lily's house. They smiled and the children waved. Lily came to the door and ushered me inside where her mother was struggling to get out of her armchair. Focussed on handing the flowers to the elderly woman, I was taken by surprise when Lily stretched up and kissed my cheek. The lingering effect of her soft skin and its strangely peppery aroma distracted me from what her mother was saying to me.

"I have heard a lot about you," I said holding out my hand, hoping this would fit in with whatever it was she had just said to me.

Lilly's mother spoke only basic English, she said, but it was easy to see where Lily got her modesty from. We spent a pleasant half-hour talking partly in French about life in general – my life in England and why I came to Africa – before the subject of Lily's mother's illness came up. She had a spinal tumour, which initially they needed to do a biopsy on to find out whether or not it was benign. If it were benign it could be removed, all well and good, and if not, she would need further treatment. Almost certainly radiotherapy and perhaps chemotherapy.

The cost of the initial treatment was mentioned casually, although it caused Lily some discomfort. I felt sad for this, so didn't mention it again. Lily brought in some dried fruit and some biscuits followed by the mille feuilles I had brought from the patisserie. We talked happily for some time and I learned quite a lot about how Cameroon had changed over the years.

Eventually the taxi driver sounded his horn and I made ready to leave. Lily's mother gripped my hand as I said goodbye. Her hands and arms seemed so thin and wrinkled.

"The day will come when Lily and I will be able to do something for you," said Lily's mother. "You are a good man and I should not hesitate, whatever it may be."

I thanked her and met Lily by the front door.

"Now Lily," I began, "I do not want to discuss the money. I don't believe in altruism, so please accept that I am giving you this money for my benefit. It will give me great pleasure to help you and your mother and I will feel better about my life if I do. So no discussion."

I handed over the envelope and she took it. She kept her head and her eyes down. I kissed her on top of her head. Then she looked up into my eyes. I wished she hadn't. Her eyes told me that nobody had ever been this kind to her in her life and maybe nobody would be again. Tears formed in my eyes.

"I must go," I said awkwardly. "I need to pack my things, then have dinner with a man from the British High Commission. I have a six o'clock flight in the morning so I hope tonight I will sleep. I'll phone you from England to see how things go with your mother's treatment," I began walking down the path. "Oh, and I didn't see your portfolio... but never mind, I'll see it next time."

Lily waved me away, wiping her tear-streaked face. Curtains twitched in neighbouring houses as I climbed into the taxi.

*

Dinner with the diplomat from the High Commission was somewhat more thought provoking than I had expected. We spent the meal talking about western aid to the third-world and then got onto the subject of altruism. He agreed with my assertion that human beings were incapable of genuine altruism, and assured me that in his experience human beings were entirely selfish – in Africa ruthlessly so. Almost as a casual aside as we left the restaurant, he mentioned that the policewoman from the day before had been arrested. Apparently another accident had occurred with the same taxi driver. On this occasion the foreign passenger was a doctor and had found the victim to be alive and uninjured. Both the taxi driver and the woman had run off and had yet to be apprehended.

"Perhaps that scruffy lawyer will defend them," I suggested.

"I see you are beginning to understand Africa my friend," he replied.

Getting into bed later, I wondered at the kinds of lives people led that would cause them to risk being hit by a moving car in order to make money. But it was Lily and her mother who dominated my thoughts as I drifted into sleep.

*

The roads were quiet on the way to the airport the next morning, giving me time to have breakfast in the cafe before boarding the plane. The waiter was just pouring me a second cup of coffee when I saw Lily wheeling a trolley with a large parcel. I got up from the table.

"Lily!" I said, unable to hide my joy at seeing her again. "Why are you here?"

"I wanted to give you this before you left," she said, putting the heavy package down. "It's one of my sculptures. It's a small gesture. I wanted to give it to you yesterday to say thank you, but I needed to get a customs certificate and have it packaged first – you'll have to wait until you get home to see it I'm afraid."

"Please sit down and have some breakfast with me," I said. "I have fifteen minutes and it would be lovely to spend even a few minutes more with you."

"David I'm so sorry, I really have to rush back," she said between breaths, "I have to work early today."

I cringed at the mention of her work. The thought of her being anywhere near to that detestable man felt like I was being stabbed in the stomach. How could I just go home and let her return to that same terrible life? Yes I had already helped her by helping her mother, but what about Lily herself? It was her I really wanted to help.

"Lily, I really don't want you to go back to working for that guy," I said. "I want you to get a catalogue of your work made – I will pay for it – and then I'll market your work in London. I don't know why I didn't think of it before. I'm more than capable of doing that. I have plenty of contacts."

Lily stood there silently, her heart pounding. I handed her the plastic envelope with the extra money I had got from the bank.

"This will be plenty to cover your expenses for now, but I'll send you more when you send me your bank details. Close your mouth or something will fly in. Get the catalogue printed, or just send me good quality photographs with something written about you and your work and I will get it done in London. Damn, I must go now or I'll miss my flight."

Lily seemed unable to reply, but there was no time to be persuasive.

"Look I'll call you when I get home," I said, paying the waiter. "Just remember what I've told you to do."

"Thank you so much," she said, quietly.

"No need to thank me," I said, making my way to the gate, "I see it as a good investment."

Buckling my seatbelt, I relaxed into my seat and opened the in-flight magazine. I had hoped for a calm departure with plenty of time, as was my habit, but it had been rushed. Not that I was unhappy to have found a possible solution to Lily's problems of course.

*

The flight was long and uncomfortable. We were delayed over an hour at take-off. Next to me sat a very large Egyptian man who insisted on spilling over into my seat. I found myself squashed up against my armrest, trying to eat with my tray turned sideways. Later the fat man fell asleep on my shoulder, snoring loudly. There seemed to be no empty places to move to. I felt uncomfortable with the idea of asking the man to move over. Using facial expressions, I tried to indicate to the flight attendants that I was unhappy with the situation but they would not take the hint. Consequently I had to suffer in silence for the full nine hours of the trip. I disembarked in London around midnight, feeling exhausted and angry. Imagine how devastated I felt, therefore, when I arrived at the immigration hall to see only three of the twenty-five desks open and three enormous queues of disgruntled fellow passengers.

Two and a half hours later I finally reached the desk. Naturally I had chosen the slowest of the three queues. The immigration official on the desk sensed my dissatisfaction. I presented my passport. Just a few more seconds, I told myself, and I could collect my baggage. Before I knew it, I would be asleep in the back of a taxi.

"Where have you travelled from today sir?" said the woman.

"Douala, Cameroon," I replied. I looked at my watch. "Yesterday actually. A nightmare journey."

The woman looked over beyond my shoulder and raised her hand. I turned and saw another woman coming towards us. She looked rather serious.

"Sir, I am sorry to ask, but could you please come with me and please bring your hand luggage."

"What seems to be the problem?" I asked, trying not to sound irritated.

"Just follow me please sir," she said, "it's only a formality."

It may only have been a formality to her, but I was exhausted. Other passengers had also begun whispering to each other, causing me some embarrassment. I followed the woman across the immigration hall. After a little awkwardness, the other queues parted to let us through. Waiting for a barrier to be opened, I sighed with frustration. Would I ever get home, I wondered?

Along a corridor I followed the woman's clicking heels until finally I was ushered into a room. She closed the door. Two other officials were waiting at a table.

"Look I'm very tired," I said. "What's all this about,

if you don't mind me asking?"

I was furious by now but still trying to remain polite.

The two male officials said nothing but opened a door, indicating that I should go through ahead of them. On a pair of long tables was the contents of my suitcase, scattered about rather like a house that had been burgled. The case seemed to have been cut open in several places.

"What the hell!" I gasped.

Slowly I took in the scene. The sculpture was there, lying on its side on the other table. The base of it had been prised open to reveal bags of white powder, packed tightly into a large cavity.

"I know nothing about this," I said immediately. "The sculpture was a present from a friend in Douala. She gave it to me at the airport this morning."

"Yes sir. You won't mind me pointing out to you will you, that this is what all drug smugglers say."

"How... how dare you!" I spluttered "I am not a drug smuggler, I'm a respectable art dealer and..."

Sarcastically the man put out both hands as if making a presentation.

"The evidence speaks for itself I think sir!"

The two women who had brought me in remained quiet during the questioning. Meanwhile one of the men was taking copious notes on a spiral pad. Not that any questions had been asked yet, I realised. Soon, however, they would ask who had given the sculpture to me. I could not for one minute think that Lily had been responsible for this situation – not at all. No, far more likely to have been some scam worked by Keita. I had no energy left, yet I was painfully aware that I had to pull myself together in order to present myself credibly. I was not naïve as to the workings of the law and it's enforcement agencies, I told myself. I watched television. I read books.

"Now look here," I began, "first and foremost I insist that I am innocent of any crime. I am the victim of a deception. Secondly, if it is your intention to make charges against me, I demand to have my solicitor present. That, I believe, is my right."

The two men looked at each other and raised their eyebrows.

"It would seem," said one of the men, turning to his colleague "that you are a bit of an old hand at this then sir. Clearly we're dealing with a professional, Clive."

Clive, the accomplice, fixed me with the kind of piercing look I thought he probably practised in a mirror.

"I think in that case, Belinda," smirked the first man, drawing the attention of one of the two women, "you'd better call Hounslow and tell them we're detaining this one. Likely as not he'll be known by some of the agencies. Better order him some breakfast for later while you're at it. Oh and get me some rubber gloves."

My heart sank. I was fit to drop and they knew it. It was under circumstances like these, I warned myself, that suspects could be encouraged to admit to anything. Stretching my fingers then clasping them hard behind my neck I made another attempt to pull myself together.

"You'll smile on the other side of your face when you find out who I really am, young man." I retorted. "Make the most of it while you can, your smugness will be short lived!"

Interlocking the fingers of his own two puffy hands, the second man turned them backwards, causing the joints to crack.

"So do you have a name for the person who gave you this... what shall we call it, this gift, sir – I presume it was a woman?"

I hesitated. "A man actually." The words seemed to come out without me realising. "Vincent. Vincent Keita. He's an art dealer in Douala. He met me by surprise at the airport this morning saying he'd forgotten to give it to me the day before. Now I come to think of it, I did think it odd at the time that he insisted I didn't unwrap it until I got home."

*

At some point I became aware that the ringing in my ears was not a part of my dream. It was the sound of my own front doorbell. I half-opened one eye. Slowly I collected my thoughts and realised where I was. After nearly two days of questioning and hours spent with my solicitor along with a man from the High Commission of Cameroon, I had finally been allowed to go home. I had been in desperate need of sleep. Despite it dawning upon me by then that the circumstances of meeting Lily, the sick mother and the wrapped gift at the airport were all part of a rather familiar cliché, I still found it hard to believe she could be responsible. Victor Keita had protested his innocence they said, but I felt no sense of guilt at him having been accused and investigated. At least the police might become aware of the nasty business he was running there and the girls might be safer now. I just hoped that it wouldn't put Lily at risk of what Keita might do. But after all this and having been exonerated, I did feel a fool. More than anything, I felt alone. The truth, I could see now, was that I had allowed myself to believe that this rather attractive and talented young woman was interested in my friendship, when all she wanted was my money. Possibly she could have allowed her boss to use me to courier drugs back to London for him, I wasn't sure.

"How blind can a lonely man be," I murmured to myself?

The ringing had turned to loud knocking. I was fully awake now. Clumsily I hunted around for a dressing gown and stumbled to my front door.

"Who is it?" I called impatiently.

"Delivery to sign for mate!" someone shouted from outside.

"Why they can't just leave it on the bloody step..." I mumbled, fumbling with the security chain. "Okay, okay, I'm coming, give me a moment!"

Eyes bleary and still half asleep I opened the door into bright sunlight. The baseball cap and overalls were a good disguise, but that peppery aroma as she hugged me was a complete give-away.

Dottie's Diary

The wind did not seem to be dying down at all and the rain was falling heavier than ever.

"So much for the weather forecast," grumbled Becca.

It was irritating. They were not those foolhardy kinds of hikers, full of naïve optimism, who set off across the moors without checking first or making suitable preparations. They were country women and they had gone to the trouble of making enquiries.

"I know," said Dottie. "Dry with a small chance of passing showers!"

They could hear the rain pounding against the roof now and the heavy slates beginning to rattle with each gust of wind. Both women were crouched down on their haunches, looking up as if the roof might come off at any moment. Becca had positioned herself against the large piece of board they had wedged against the window opening, but it too was beginning to rattle. Taking a wooden fence post from a stack in the corner, Dottie stretched to jam it between the board and one of the roof trusses. The rattling stopped.

"God you are brilliant," said Becca, relieved not to have to hold the board in place any longer. "So do you think a farmer keeps animals in here then?"

"No sign of anything larger than a mouse or a cat having been in here recently," replied Dottie, looking around.

It was certainly dry enough though. The slate roof had bowed a little in the middle and at one end the stone wall was a bit green where water regularly ran down inside, but there was a door and now that the piece of board had been wedged against the window opening, it seemed secure.

Becca moved a larger piece of board from the corner and laid it down on top of four posts to create a dry platform for them to sit on. Unfolding Dottie's picnic blanket from her backpack, the two women sat down.

"A fire'd be nice Dottie, wouldn't it?" said Becca, rubbing her hands together.

"No chimney Becs," replied Dottie, disconsolately. "We'd be bloody asphyxiated. Here eat this."

Opening her chubby white hand, Dottie revealed two squares of something.

"What is it, biscuit?" asked Becca.

"Kendal Mint Cake," said Dottie. "Steve put it in my back pack. Thought I didn't notice. He always has to take it when we walk anywhere. Boy scout thing I think. Disgusting eh?"

"I think I rather like it actually," said Becca.

"Mmm, so you be bloody married to him then. I reckon he fancies you anyway, you know!"

The two women began squealing with laughter. Even the prop falling on them when they knocked against the window board did not stop them.

"Urgh, no thanks," laughed Becca, "That beard tickling my thighs. Not my idea of fun!"

"Beard tickling your thighs?" screeched Dottie, "You'd be lucky, girl. Missionary position man, Steve!"

"Jeezus Dot, so you mean you're still doing it with him?"

They screamed with laughter again.

"Oh yes," cried Dottie, "Christmas and birthdays! Actually no, just birthdays now. Don't wan'a give him an 'art attack do I?"

Laughing so much now, the two large women rolled over and again disturbed the window board, which fell down on top of them with a crash. It hurt but it only caused them to laugh more.

Rain was lashing in through the window opening again. Eventually they calmed down enough to lift the board off them.

"Oh goodness, dreadfully sorry, I heard screaming," came a voice.

Dottie and Becca peered through the darkness. Someone... a woman, was standing in the light at the open door. Disentangling themselves from each other and from the sheet of board, they got to their feet.

"No no, please don't stop on my account," said the woman backing out of the doorway. "I heard screaming you see. Never fear ladies, I'm quite broad-minded. I'm not ignorant of country ways any more than I am about the notion of Sapphic romance, so to speak."

Rebecca and Dottie turned to look at each other, repeating the woman's words in mime.

"Sapphic romance?"

Neither of them was any the wiser.

"Look do come in, dearie" said Dottie "You'll get soaked. We're just sheltering here from the storm, see. The board we put in front of the window blew in and fell on us, y' see. That's why we was screaming."

The girls' accents always took on a broader Hampshire brogue when they were having fun.

"Yes, more laughing than screaming really," said Becca, shouting over the noise of the wind.

"I see," said the woman suspiciously. "Well I suppose it would do me no harm to get out of this beastly wind and rain."

The woman stepped inside and shut the door against the howling wind. Proffering a stiff hand she stepped forward cautiously. The three women shook hands politely. Becca even made an embarrassing attempt at a curtsey.

"Harriet. Harriet Berryman de Villalba. From Carrig Hall down the valley. My husband's South American you see. Such a pretentious name really. We're in horse breeding but never mind that now. How did you get here, dears?"

"Left the car at the station in Aberdovey and legged-it up here from there early this morning," said Dotty. "We was hoping to make it to the top of Cadair Idris and then, weather permitting, on to Aran Fawddwy. Bloody weather forecast said it'd be dry," she chuckled, "with a small chance of passing blinking showers."

Pulling away some plastic fertiliser sacks piled aganst the back wall, Harriet managed to find herself a wooden box. Placing it next to Becca and Dottie's platform, she proceeded to sit on it. She was nicely dressed. Smart jeans and a long Barbour waxed-cotton coat. Even her wellington boots looked classy.

"Oh never rely on the weather forecast for this area," laughed Harriet. "We get completely different weather here. It'll be sunny in Aberystwyth!"

"So is this your land then Harriet?" asked Becca.

"No no dear, one couldn't raise racehorses on this land. Pit ponies maybe. No I think this land belongs to Mrs Owen. Her husband died last year. A tree fell on him, poor chap. Terrible business."

"In a storm?" asked Becca.

"No, in a Landrover dear. A large oak. He was trying to pull it out with a chain, the silly man. It was blocking Mrs Owen's view of Cadair Idris. It fell straight on the Landrover. Killed him stone dead!"

"Ooh, poor man," said Dottie. "And poor Mrs Owen."

"Oh Mrs Owen didn't mind," said Harriet. "She's got her view and her sons have come home now the father has gone. A strange business, but that's the countryside for you. Who are we to judge eh? So where are you ladies from – I mean where do you live?"

"Andover," said the two women. "Hampshire."

"My husband's in chickens," said Dottie. "Becca's still single – at forty-something! I'm only jealous."

"I have a boyfriend, thank you!" laughed Becca.

"Don't listen to her, she has several," said Dottie.

"But I thought you two were..." began Harriet nervously.

"What?" asked Dottie, smiling awkwardly. "You thought we were what?"

Becca and Dottie looked each other up and down, wondering what it was about them that might have given them the appearance of being anything in particular.

"Well you know, I thought you were together. I heard the squealing and the giggling, then I looked inside and saw you... well you know, cuddling, and I..."

"Oh my God, no! You thought we were..." Becca didn't want to say it in case she was wrong.

"Yes dear, lesbians. We do get them down here you know." Harriet laughed casually.

"Oh God no!" said Dottie, chuckling. "We like men. I mean we do it with men, we don't like 'em all that much, but we don't do it with women. Least I don't!"

Becca looked at Dottie uncomfortably and then at Harriet.

"I'm not fussy, she's trying to say, Harriet. It's just a joke between us," said Becca, looking like her feelings had been hurt.

"So what's your husband like in the sack then, Harriet?" said Dottie, sniggering and quickly covering her mouth. "Mine's a bloody disaster!"

Harriet's mouth fell open.

"Don't listen to her, Harriet," said Becca, pushing her

friend away. "She's got a mischievous streak. Almost Tourette's really. She just comes out with stuff."

"No," said Dottie, "really, I'm interested. I had an Argentinian boyfriend when I did apple picking. Near Winchester, one summer after school. Juan his name was. We stayed in mobile homes for the summer. He was a demon in bed and romantic with it, I tell you. I often think about him. Just wondering if he was a one off?"

Harriet was smiling. "Well, what should I say? Alfredo's Argentinian. The first thing is about half the male Argentinian population are named Juan. But you're quite right actually, Dottie. Not that I've had… experiences with other Argentinian men, but going by what I see and what I hear amongst the women when I'm there, Argentinian men are indeed very hot blooded and also inclined to be rather romantic, they say."

"Listen," said Becca, "the rain's stopped."

Opening the door, Harriet poked her head out. The wind had dropped a little too.

"Hmm, there are still some nasty looking black clouds coming this way," said Harriet. "I wouldn't advise continuing up to the top of Cadair Idris today. My car is just down the hill. I've got to collect some eggs from Mrs Owen, then why don't I take you ladies back to The Hall for afternoon tea? If we go now we might just avoid a soaking."

Clutching the cartons of eggs, Becca and Dottie

luxuriated in the back seat of Harriet's Range Rover with the heater blowing on their muddy legs. The dark clouds were gathering at the head of the valley and they could already see the rain coming down hard, further down. The two visitors looked down at their scruffy attire, concerned about how they would be taken at The Hall.

"We've trodden mud into your lovely car I'm afraid, Harriet," said Dottie.

"It's what it's for dear," said Harriet. "Alfredo will get one of the boys to deal with it after we get back."

Passing through the ornate electric gates and clattering over the cattle grids, they made their way up Harriet's long drive, Dottie and Becca raising eyebrows at each other.

"You know I could always get one of the boys to go and fetch your car for you, come to think of it," said Harriet as they climbed out.

No sooner had they removed themselves from the car than people arrived, looking busy. One young woman took the eggs to the kitchen. A young man arrived and took the keys from Harriet. Dottie and Becca presumed he was about to attend to the mud in the rear foot-well.

"Take off your boots and one of the boys will clean them," said Harriet. "Coats go on the pegs. There are house slippers in the box there. All sizes. Just help yourselves. I think we'll go through to the orangery Cristina. Tea and scones I think. Orange pekoe. It'll be fun to watch the storm from a dry warm place, eh ladies? Oh and Cristina, please ask Mr Villalba to join us. He'll be in his study."

Dottie and Becca giggled uncomfortably, their eyes everywhere. To think that fifteen or twenty minutes ago they were sharing a cowshed with the lady of this house. Of all this!

Sitting in Harriet's orangery was, they imagined, something like one of those grand hotels at a hill-station in 1920's India. It would not have surprised them to see a Maharaja or a finely dressed Prince sitting waiting for them.

"Such a beautiful place to live, Harriet," said Dottie.

"Oh thank you dear, it does us fine," said Harriet. "Bizarrely Alfredo likes the cool climate and the storms, while I miss the sun in Argentina. The grass is always greener, as they say."

There was a clinking noise and the two visitors turned to see Cristina and an older lady with a pair of large oval trays.

"Orange Pekoe tea madam and freshly baked scones. Chef thought they might be appreciated what with the weather madam," said the older lady.

"Lovely. How thoughtful of him. Thank you Olivia. Now do you have everything you want, ladies?"

Becca and Dottie assured Harriet that they did. The

tea was poured and scones served with fresh clotted cream and homemade strawberry jam. Suddenly there was a crack, followed by a crash of thunder across the gardens. It startled them.

"Good afternoon ladies," came a voice from behind them.

"Ah Alfredo, just in time for tea," said Harriet. "Dear, I found these poor ladies sheltering in a cowshed, up on the mountain near Mrs Owen's. This is Becca and Dottie."

Alfredo stepped forward to shake hands.

"Well, what good luck! I'm honoured to meet such intrepid ladies. I am Alfredo, the long-suffering husband."

The two women laughed, politely. Becca rose to her feet and was about to perform another curtsey when she was restrained by Dottie.

"Harriet rescued us," said Dottie, self-consciously.

"Oh hardly dears. I'm sure you'd have managed fine without me," said Harriet.

"Your house is magnificent," said Becca. "The sort of place I remember dreaming of living as a girl."

"Yes it's lovely," said Alfredo. "It's my wife's family house really. She grew up here."

"His father told him he was so lazy, his only chance

of maintaining the luxury he had become used to at home, was to marry a rich older woman," laughed Harriet.

"Ah yes, it's true," said Alfredo, smiling, "I think he hoped it would... spur me on to prove him wrong. He underestimated me! Anyway you're not so much older my dear."

Harriet laughed, reassuring her visitors that she bore no resentment to her husband for his jokes.

"Yes, I can afford to laugh, dears, said Harriet. Fortunately for me, Alfredo's instinctive abilities in horse breeding have brought me more than the value of this old house several times over."

"Ha ha, she exaggerates!" replied Alfredo, clapping his smooth hands together. "So I presume by your accents, that you ladies are not from Wales. Have you come far?" asked Alfredo, accepting his cup of orange pekoe from Cristina.

"Hampshire," replied Becca, "Andover."

"Hampshire, really!" said Alfredo, raising an eyebrow. "A great horse breeding area. I know it well."

"Do you?" chimed all three ladies in harmony.

"Of course. I was there as part of my equestrian studies. I was in Stockbridge. Just up the road from you really."

"Stockbridge?" said Dottie, a note of surprise in her

voluptuous voice.

"Bugger!" muttered Dottie.

"Yes," said Alfredo, "It's a big racehorse breeding centre. More in the past than now perhaps, but I'm sure you know that."

"Yes that's right," said Becca. "Surely you know that, Dottie?"

"Yes, I do thank you," replied Dottie, who had begun fiddling with her hair.

They waited, but Dottie did not continue. Taking a large gulp of her tea, she walked over to the table. As the cup rattled on the saucer, threatening to topple, the others watched her with a sense of nervous anticipation. Her behaviour was quite out of character, Becca thought.

"Uhm, well isn't this lovely, is someone going to have a scone? I adore scones, don't you Becca?" said Dottie excitedly.

Cristina immediately stepped forward to help her and an uncomfortable little transaction took place with each of them unsure who should do what. Surprised by her friend's uncharacteristic awkwardness, Becca moved into the arena and took a plate, hoping to draw attention away from Dottie and Cristina. The atmosphere was becoming a little tense.

"Delicious looking strawberry jam!" said Becca, her enthusiasm a little overblown. "Do you make it yourself?"

"Chef makes it, doesn't he Cristina?" said Harriet. "From strawberries he gets over near Aberystwyth?"

"Yes madam," mumbled Cristina.

"How lovely," said Becca.

Still the others remained silent. Becca was finding it increasingly difficult to make all the conversation.

"Erm, apparently, Dottie had an Argentinian boyfriend for a summer, back in Hampshire, is that right Dottie?"

Again Becca overcooked the enthusiasm in her voice. This time, however, it had an effect on the reticence of the others.

"Becca!" gasped Dottie.

"What?" replied Becca. "You mentioned it quite happily earlier on."

"Yes but that was..." Again Dottie thought better of finishing her sentence. "Uhm, is there any more tea?"

Pouring more hot water into the delicate porcelain teapot from an ornate silver pot, Cristina agitated the tea.

"Cuidado, Cristina, por favour!" said Harriet, alarmed.

But she had spoken too late. A shower of tea shot out

of the pot and over the neatly pressed white linen tablecloth.

"Oi madre mia!" cried Cristina. "Siempre tan stupida... I go to take a cloth from kitchen madam. Sorry, very sorry madam."

"It's alright, Cristina," said Harriet, placing her hands gently on the girl's shoulders. "It can wait until later. Go and get on with the laundry. I'll be mother."

Calmly, Harriet poured Dottie her tea as Cristina disappeared from the room, sniffing.

"There now, who else would like a second cup?"

"Er, not for me," said Alfredo. "I have some administrative things to deal with."

"Oh no, Alfredo," insisted Harriet, "surely that can wait? I wanted to hear more about Dottie's Argentinian boyfriend. We need your comments on Argentinian men."

"Well, I suppose..." began Alfredo, reluctantly.

"Please Dottie, do tell us," said Harriet. "For Alfredo's benefit you should begin with why you were there."

"Oh no it's boring really."

The others waited patiently. They were not in the slightest bit bored.

"Well… it was a long time ago," began Dottie, reluctantly. "I'd only just finished school. I hardly remember it."

"Oh come off it Dottie," laughed Becca, "you remembered quite a lot earlier in the cowshed! You know Harriet thought we were a pair of lesbians, Alfredo?"

Becca was not at all sure how this last piece of information had managed to slip out. There was such a tense atmosphere. It was usually Dottie who could be relied upon to blurt out inappropriate things. Alfredo's face was a picture of surprise.

"Really! What were the circumstances to make her believe this?" asked Alfredo, smiling and sitting back down. "Actually you know dear I think I will have another cup of tea."

Harriet made a tut tutting sound and shook her head.

"You men. Sometimes I think you are more fond of gossip than women are! It was just a joke really. The wind had blown over a piece of board that the girls had wedged in front of the open window. It had fallen on top of them and they were grappling about underneath it as I came in. I think that's right isn't it?" Harriet turned to Becca. "Anyway, we've drifted off the subject. What *was* the name of your Argentinian boyfriend, Dottie?"

"I… I don't remember," said Dottie. "As I said it was so long ago."

"But didn't you say it was Juan?" said Becca.

"I might have done. But I'm really not sure," replied Dottie, wiping strawberry jam from her lip.

"So did you know any Argentinian young men named Juan around Stockbridge when you were there, Alfredo," asked Harriet, "it must have been around the same time, come to think of it?"

"Hmm... let me think... No, no I don't remember any my dear. But like Dottie says we are talking about many years ago, no?"

"Oh come, come, Alfredo," said Harriet. "Alfredo has an excellent memory, ladies. Surely you'd remember, Alfredo. I think Dottie said earlier that the young man was a true romantic and... well... quite the Casanova!"

Becca sniggered. Alfredo had begun shuffling his feet, searching his memory, or so it seemed. Clearly Alfredo was uncomfortable, but Harriet was not about to let the matter go.

"Perhaps you think me so old, Alfredo," said Harriet, "that I've forgotten that one of your middle names is Juan or that you used to use this name when you were a boy? I seem to remember that your cousin Manolo, still calls you Juan in fact. Do correct me if I'm wrong."

Alfredo sighed deeply. He should have known better than to try to pull the wool over Harriet's eyes. Dottie, meanwhile, had transformed from a confident, outspoken young Hampshire countrywoman, to a shy, red-faced girl. Making every attempt to disappear into the background, she wrung her hands and kept her eyes firmly on the floor.

"Forgive me," said Alfredo, "in my culture it is considered gentlemanly to spare the embarrassment of a lady with whom one has had a previous...er, liaison. And I was not sure at first. I was not sure about her name either."

A small whimpering sound was heard from the corner Dottie had retreated to.

"Oh please don't worry, Dottie dear." said Harriet, walking over and placing a reassuring arm around her shoulder. "I'm so sorry. It's about Alfredo, not you. I've been working on getting him to be more candid about things. Just my little pet peeve really. He has a tendency to pussyfoot around issues without good reason. Personally I feel gentlemanliness is a poor excuse for deceit. I don't say this unkindly, Alfredo, as you know. But in this instance I feel a lot of discomfort could have been avoided if you could just have said that you remembered Dottie, when you first realised it."

"Very well, Harriet," sighed Alfredo, lowering the tone of his voice. "If this is the way it must be for you." Alfredo sighed deeply. "Am I right in thinking, Dottie, that when you were younger you were known as Dorothy?"

There was another small whimper from Dottie as she

walked over to the windows. The rain was still lashing down. There was a croaking sound and a cough as Dottie tried to reply.

"H'hum… my parents still call me Dorothy," said Dottie. "Yes I did call myself Dorothy back then."

"Well how lovely to have reacquainted the two of you then?" said Harriet, without a hint of sarcasm. "How long is it?"

"Twenty one years this summer," said Alfredo. "How long after did you marry, Dorothy?"

"Oh a while after. Steve and I met at agricultural college as mature students about six or seven years after that summer."

"And you stayed in caravans, Dottie was saying earlier, is that right?" asked Becca, trying hard to diffuse the tension in the conversation.

"Well I used to travel backwards and forwards from Stockbridge at first," said Alfredo, "but then after Dorothy… Dottie and I got together, I used to stay there, yes."

Dottie remained staring out at the rain. She was still uncharacteristically quiet.

"So you were both around… what seventeen, eighteen?" asked Harriet.

"I'm not sure," said Alfredo. "I must have been around…"

"Twenty," said Dottie, her voice more assured. "I was sixteen, nearly seventeen."

"Young!" remarked Harriet. "Very young."

"Things were different in those days," said Alfredo, awkwardly. "Especially in the country."

"Hmm... in Hampshire perhaps," replied Harriet, smiling.

"I was a bit innocent actually," said Dottie. "My mum and dad were pretty strict and old fashioned so I didn't have much experience with boys before that."

"So you were a virgin then Dottie?" asked Harriet bluntly.

"Well, mm, I suppose I was. I mean, yes I was."

Dottie had turned to face them all now. Becca had never seen her friend behave shyly. She was usually so matter-of-fact, especially about sex. In fact most people they knew found her shocking. If she folded and unfolded her napkin much more, Becca thought, it was going to fall apart.

"Did you know Dottie was a virgin at the time, Alfredo?" asked Harriet.

Alfredo knew his wife was still testing his candidness. He got to his feet and pretended to be brushing scone crumbs off the tablecloth.

"She told me later, I think," said Alfredo.

"After the second time," said Dottie.

"Ah, you have a good memory too, Dottie," laughed Alfredo uncomfortably.

"I have a diary for every year from seven until I was eighteen."

"Really?" said Becca, amazed. "So all the details are there then?"

"The important ones, yes."

"Like the times you made love?" asked Harriet.

"Harriet, darling, I don't think..." began Alfredo nervously.

"I don't mind," said Dottie. "I'm over the embarrassment now. I think I was worried about making Harriet feel uncomfortable, but I can see I was wrong about that."

"So without going into detail, Dottie," said Becca, sniggering, "I presume it says whether you enjoyed it – the diary I mean – like how many times, techniques and all that?"

"More about quantity than quality if I remember correctly," replied Dottie. "I don't think I had the words to describe it much back then anyway."

Harriet, Dottie and Becca were together now in their lack of discomfort with the topic. Alfredo on the other hand, as hard as he tried to indicate the opposite, was obviously in agony. He remained shuffling his feet and pacing about, hoping perhaps that something might soon occur to divert them from these awkward recollections. Another teapot incident maybe? Alfredo moved towards the pot.

"Oookay then... so no descriptions, but I'm wondering, does Dottie's Diary have a record of how many times?" asked Becca, cheekily.

"It might have," said Dottie, smiling coyly.

"No no, don't tell us Dottie," said Harriet playfully. Let's see how good Alfredo's memory is, shall we? Alfredo, how many times do you think the young Juan – or Don Juan, perhaps we should call him under the circumstances – how many times do you think he and the young Dorothy made love? Just a guess."

Becca sniggered. Meanwhile, rocking from foot to foot, hands in pockets, Alfredo mumbled to himself. This continued for longer than Harriet felt was polite.

"We're not asking you to relive each occasion in your mind, Alfredo, dear!"

At this Becca burst into fits of laughter. Dottie was also amused by the comment. Alfredo too began to laugh, albeit uncomfortably.

"Well," he began, " I suppose... hm... hm, five, six... nine... I think probably around twenty. Maybe twenty two."

Harriet and Becca immediately turned to Dottie. Trying to appear casual, as if they might be talking about the number of times they had drunk tea together. Alfredo was again pacing about the room.

"Well Dottie, is he close?" asked Harriet.

"I may be overestimating. It might have been less, I'm not sure... eighteen?" mumbled Alfredo.

"Seventy-four," said Dottie. "Seventy four if you don't count the…"

"Seventy f…four!" Coughed Alfredo. "Are you sure?"

"Positive," said Dottie.

"So… over how long is that?" asked Harriet, "Six months, a year?"

"A month," said Dottie. "Four weeks in fact."

"Alfredo!" said Harriet, "But that's an average of nearly… three times a day for a month!"

"I was young!" said Alfredo. "I am Argentinian. I wasn't trying to break a record! What do you want me to say? She was a very sexy girl. Beautiful!"

The sound of the words, "thank you," were barely audible, but they all read them on Dottie's lips.

Somewhat insensitive to the feelings of the others, Becca lost control at this point and was soon roaring with laughter.

*

The rain had slowed by the time Alfredo dropped the women at the station car park. In a relatively short time, a firm friendship had been forged between them and Harriet. They were less sure about Alfredo. He seemed stiff and pensive during the drive into town, trying to make conversation about the weather, flooding and the sinkholes. Somehow he managed to make it last the whole way there. He kissed both of them politely as they stood, about to get into their car, but his kisses lacked the warmth of Harriet's parting embrace back at The Hall. Like the true gentleman Alfredo was, he waited to see that their car started safely and then made his own way home.

"Well I can't say I could ever have imagined any of that happening before we set out yesterday, Dottie," said Becca, "can you?"

Dottie didn't need to answer, she just laughed and shook her head in disbelief.

"Seventy-four times in four weeks woman?" exclaimed Becca. "What are you a girl or a rabbit?"

"I was inquisitive," said Dottie. "To be honest I didn't know what was normal either. For all I knew then, all grown-ups did it three times a day!"

The rain began falling harder again as they pulled out of the station car park and a fork of lightening lit up the sky behind the hills. The rumbling thunder that followed was long, like an ogre's loud grumbling.

"You gonna tell Steve about it then?" asked Becca, turning to look Dottie in the eye for a moment. "About Alfredo – or Don Juan, I mean?"

"Hmm, probably not," said Dottie. "Oh I mean Steve knows about him but…"

"Yeah, probably not about the seventy-four times in four weeks though, eh?" laughed Becca. "And I bet they weren't all missionary position either, you tart!"

The Commuter

Jolted awake, David glanced nervously around the railway carriage. Thankfully he was alone. This was a painfully familiar scenario these days. He had been asleep with his mouth hanging open; a habit he had tried hard to overcome, but with little success. Taking out his neatly folded handkerchief he wiped away a rivulet of drool. Long resigned to self-disgust, he consoled himself with the fact that at least on this occasion nobody had seen. Appearances still mattered to him, however worthless his life had become.

Tiredness was his constant companion nowadays. He had been working long hours ever since he could remember; you might say it had come to define him. For years he had returned home after his wife was asleep and got up long before she awoke, until one day she wasn't there anymore. Regrettable now – losing her – but as a man with a tidy mind he was regularly reassured by the symmetry he recognised in its inevitability.

Rising to his feet David slid open the small window, cringing as his joints protested. Somehow he had felt sure the window would be jammed shut. They usually were. Life had a habit of treating him that way. It was a cool autumn evening and the carriage was rather overheated, so the breeze was a welcome relief. He slumped back into his seat, his gaze still fixed on the train window, although there was nothing to see outside. The odd light appeared in the distance then a blur of some cars waiting at a level crossing. The carriage rocked and clattered. Catching his reflection looking back at him from the dark, he was reminded of how old he had become. Where was that man full of hope and the love of life who once rode this train, he wondered? Regrettably David realised he couldn't recall that young face at all. A lifetime spent on a bloody train line! And for what? He had no answers. On this point the symmetry eluded him. But these thoughts of regret were so familiar to him. Lost years that he had never had the courage to do anything about. How pathetic he felt. He dozed off again.

Bored with its own mundane clatter, the train began to slow. It almost seemed to have given up. As if it had been accused of being complicit in this passenger's wasted life. Very gradually it coasted to a halt. David's eyes opened. Sleep had not placed any better complexion upon things. In the stillness, he now saw his grey reflection more clearly, his frown accentuating a deeply furrowed brow and crow's feet around the eyes. The silence disturbed him; it felt unnatural. It was as if the entire world had stopped. He sat motionless, looking at this face, staring deeper into himself. His life, like his repetitive journeys home, were utterly predictable. And yet he found it all so inexplicable.

Just at that moment, in the blackness somewhere beyond his reflection, David saw something moving – a flickering light. He leaned closer to the window trying to see what was out there. Identifying various elements in the middle distance one by one, he struggled to make sense of the scene. Mysterious, he thought. The train remained still and silent. Then all of a sudden something startled him, causing him to pull back from the window with a gasp. For a second the light had caught the face of a man. A man who was close to the carriage. He glanced behind him in case it was another reflection. It was not. Were people about to try and board the train, he wondered? He was also now aware of a strange smell of burning oil. Reaching slowly into his jacket pocket, he put on his glasses in hope of a better view. Cautiously he brought his face back close to the glass, holding his breath to avoid fogging it. Little by little the scene started to become clearer to him – his mind hurriedly trying to take it in. An anxiety that the train might restart at any second had also begun to trouble him

What was happening here, he asked himself? Little more than a few feet away from where he stood the ragged concrete image of a wall began to form – the wall of the railway embankment close to where it entered a tunnel. It seemed to him that at some point in the past there must have been an electrical installation in that wall, which had since been removed. It had left behind a large crevice. A busy pavement with railings ran just a few feet above the crevice. Indeed, he caught the lower half of a number of pedestrians hurrying past in those first few moments. But it was the crevice itself that held his interest. His heart began pounding as he realised that he was looking at the figure of a semi-naked man, sitting in the crevice, glowing in the light of a simple oil lamp. Undisturbed by the train, the man was writing in a large notebook, lying on a mattress. Bizarrely, the bed was properly made up, with clean sheets and a maroon coloured quilt that partly covered him.

Something about this young man's face was familiar to David; something from the past, but he couldn't remember what. The young man did not attempt to hide himself. Neither did he look dirty or unwell. This did not fit, therefore, with the obvious explanation of him being a vagrant. A dense bough of ivy and a heavy cut-velvet curtain offered the man privacy, although both had been drawn aside. On the inner wall of the cell, he noticed that the man had carefully fixed a few pictures. David could see clearly that one of them was an illustration of Jesus distributing loaves and fishes. The others seemed to be old family photographs.

The oil lamp David had first seen flickering was placed on a small makeshift wooden shelf fixed alongside the man's head, and beside it was a bottle of fountain pen ink. Next to that stood a small crystal glass of what may have been wine or port. David was so close that he could see the light catching the fair hair on the young man's slender arm, yet the young man seemed as oblivious to him as he was to the train or the crisp night air. David's eyes moved along the man's arm, over his antiquated wristwatch, and then lingered at the thin fingers gently holding the notebook. The fingers were not those of a man accustomed to hardship; they appeared clean and soft and the nails well shaped. The young man revolved his wrist slightly to turn the book more into the light and as he did so, the eye of his solitary observer darted back to the old watch. For some reason David had noticed that it showed the wrong time. Attention to detail was his forte. In fact he was sure that the watch had stopped. His heart raced alarmingly, but this time he did not pull back. His stare remained fixed on that watch, as if he knew it held the answer to all this – the reason the man was there in that crevice, and why *he* was here on this train. He wanted to know why. So little aroused David's curiosity these days, but this he felt he had to know.

Without warning a metallic screech shattered the stillness. There was a jolt and the train began rolling forwards. Uncharacteristically panicked by his impending loss, David jumped to his feet and slammed both hands against the window. He was in a cold sweat and his hands left imprints on the glass, but the glowing young man continued, oblivious and undisturbed, writing with a beautiful flowing movement, taking the utmost care with the formation of each individual letter. Yet the writing on the page was agonisingly out of view. It seemed important to David to know what the man was writing – vital in fact, but the illuminated scene was sliding slowly away.

"No, no please," he murmured, "please wait!"

David's repeated words grew louder and he began banging his fists on the glass with increasing desperation. "Who are you?" he called out, as the scene threatened to move out of view. Things were fading back into blackness. Then just at that moment, as if he had known the passenger was there all along, the young man looked up. He looked straight into David's eyes, and then he said something, holding out his hand. Slowly, agonisingly, the man disappeared from view.

David collapsed onto the seat, exhausted by the intensity of the experience. What had the man said? Something about the light, he thought. He was so transfixed that he had not thought of running down the train to keep the young man in view for longer; long enough perhaps, to discern more from the man's lips. How would he solve the riddle now? He was exhausted, like a man who had lost a long battle. His tearful eyes closed.

But no sooner had David relaxed, when in an instant he was torn back to reality as the interconnecting carriage door slid heavily open. The conductor marched past, sniffing the air. Hesitating on his way, he glanced down at the ashen-faced passenger, who he noticed was crying.

"Are you all right sir?" said the old conductor, placing a caring hand on David's shoulder. "I thought I heard someone shouting."

The conductor spoke with a clear, surprisingly cultured voice, reminiscent of an army officer. He seemed particularly approachable.

"I saw... I saw a man!" gasped David. "Out of the window."

He looked away, back out into the dark. Then his voice grew more distant. "He beckoned to me, but... his watch. It had stopped you see."

The conductor stiffened, looking seriously into David's uncomprehending eyes. Only for a moment, though it seemed uncomfortably long. Finally he exhaled and spoke, cautiously.

"You needn't worry about it at all sir. Just relax. It's rather like time itself you see. No no. There's no point trying to make sense of something when we can't change it, mark my words sir. No point at all."

David's gaze returned to the darkness. The conductor had not really answered his questions. He felt patronised. Almost as if the conductor thought it was beyond David's comprehension. He was feeling increasingly strange – unwell perhaps. The carriage seemed to have grown cold and drained of all its colour somehow. He was being seized by an overwhelming conviction that he belonged out there, with the glowing man and his broken watch. There was no doubt in his mind, he would have to find his way back there. As soon as he had the energy.

"But... so what's the point of it then," asked David, weakly, "if we can't make sense of it? How do we even know it's real?"

Turning his head, David addressed the conductor, but the conductor had gone. Sighing he allowed his head to fall back against the seat. Tired of searching for answers his body relaxed at last.

*

"Excuse me mate, end of the line I'm afraid," said a young man, rubbish sack in hand.

But David remained still. He was not asleep. His wet eyes were open, but unblinking.

"Sir?"

The Line of Fire

Clinging precariously to life in the war-torn trouble spot I once called home, I reconsidered my options. The whole bloody area was a minefield and I was constantly watched. So why was I still here? Surely any sensible person would have taken flight ages ago? And that was my dilemma. Although I was undoubtedly the enemy, my continued presence seemed required. Presumably I had not suffered sufficiently. Eternal persecution seemed to be my lot. The challenge therefore, was to remain but to survive. Either that or end it all myself, and I knew I wouldn't do that. There was no justice here. My human rights counted for nothing. The Peacekeepers did little to protect me. They even seemed to hold me partly responsible. No, if I was to survive, my only chance was to stay out of the line of fire.

*

I think it was the smell of cedar that drew me to the

option of the shed. A fragile bunker though it was, it gave me a warm feeling inside. I'd built it in happier times, before the war. It was tucked away out of sight, but a soft target nonetheless. It was a tactical dilemma but I needed to act quickly and in the end gut instinct prevailed.

I spent the morning cleaning and removing junk. Spiders had taken it over and they were reluctant to be evicted. I managed to remove a few with a newspaper but some of them had to be trodden on. The similarity of their situation to my own was painfully apparent to me but it felt like "kill or be killed". Finally I laid an old Moroccan rug on the floor, got a barrow and fetched a narrow sofa-bed, desk, clothes and some hurriedly selected books. I had just managed to drag a barrel of water and box of tinned food inside when I heard the gate.

I was sitting at my desk, writing, when she came in.

"Darling, what are you doing? You've made it lovely down here."

I didn't dare look up. I felt disarmed; she had not called me darling for months. I mumbled something pacifistic about giving her space.

"Mm, I rather like this arrangement," she said, using that cheeky, childish voice that she thought I found endearing.

Surely this was a preamble to an attack I thought?

She walked over to the bed, noticing the old cotton blanket we had bought when backpacking in India. She sighed as she breathed in the musty aroma.

"God that takes me back."

Her voice seemed changed. Compassion, it sounded like...

Unconvinced, I maintained my guard. I heard the bed creak. She didn't invite further conversation, nor did I offer any. I continued writing – happy for the ceasefire yet expecting a renewed onslaught at any moment.

*

Time passed slowly. The buzzing of a bee against my newly cleaned windows and the soft scratching of my pen the only sounds. I studied the sleeping tiger. How safe a retreat was this now, I wondered?

I don't know how long I watched her for. After a time the sun cast a warm shaft that caught the downy hair on her neck. That almost heart-shaped scar on her forehead where she had slipped off a gangplank in Bali. Dreaming, I drifted on a Javanese sea until a breeze moved the branch of the overhanging walnut tree, rattling the shingled roof. Her lashes quivered and opened. She smiled, waving me towards her. I still remembered that look. Surely not?

*

We lay there silently afterwards, listening to the

creaking tree, insects, children running through a field somewhere in the distance. Somehow everything seemed possible again. Even if the war restarted tomorrow it seemed worth it, just for an afternoon.

The Peacekeepers would be home from school soon. I knew one of us would have to break the silence, and in the end it was her.

"We're going to have to put some curtains up in here," she said.

The 'F' Word
A Conversation Overheard On A Train

"That's not a nice thing to say and it's going to get you to bed when we get home."

"I didn't say *that*!"

"A tea with milk please. What do you children want? Quickly please! You can have one thing each. Tell the man, he's waiting."

"Quavers! Quavers!"

"Yes, and me, Quavers!"

"And me, Quavers!"

"Quavers what?"

"Quavers please!"

"Okay, three packets of Quavers and two cups of tea please. Take your feet off the chair."

*

"Anyway I was thinking I could cut up the bread first then make a bit of a picnic, you know it would be nice, put it all in a bag and take it with us to the... what is it Daniel, Mummy's talking?"

"No, a question! Mum what's this?"

"I don't know, what is it?"

"Hah, it's a look!"

"Hmm...Play with Gideon please Daniel. So anyway, as I was saying, I looked but I didn't have one, or at least I couldn't find one."

"You shouldn't talk with your mouth full Gideon it's not p'lite."

"Shut up Lilly you little..."

"Right that's it, give me the Quavers now, you can save some for later! Thank you. Thank you. Quickly please...thank you!"

"Mum, how will you know which one's which later?"

"Never mind that, I just will."

"Mum can I have a drink? ...Thank you. Oh, it's got ice in it!"

"Mummy she's kicking me."

"Mum, this is not kicking, look!"

"Right! Take your feet off the chair Gideon. You don't ever do what I tell you! So anyway, I gave up on looking and…"

"NOW do I? Mum! Now do I?"

"Mum! I need to…"

"What, Lilly?"

"Mum, you know. Can I?"

"When you get off the train you can Lilly."

(Mumbles)

"Could you not say that please Lilly!"

"I SAID it!"

*

"Look, I could draw a *haitch* for you Lilly. Or do you want an *eh*?"

"No, that's not an *eh*, Daniel, that's a *ger*."

"Look, this is a kicking *ker*, Lilly."

That is NOT a kicking *ker*, Gideon!

"Yes, so I thought, look in the charity shops. But then I looked in that posh shop… you know, by the bank, and they had one. It's expensive for feeding the ducks but it'll be nice."

"Now this is an *ef*, Lilly."

"Not the *ef* word?"

"Mummy, Lilly said the *ef* word."

"Thank you Gideon, now sit down and don't tell tales. Lilly! Did you say the *ef* word?"

"...Well, nearly I did!"

The Bottle Lady Of Luang Prabang

Days pass slowly, most beginning with breakfast at our street café. Today our attention is drawn by the chink of glass somewhere in the early morning traffic haze. Across the road we see a haggard woman with a handcart, collecting bottles and sorting them on a small patch of waste ground. A kitchen cupboard lays dumped there. I propose she lives in it. Comic, until she climbs inside and slides the door shut. We stare, waiting, but she stays put.

A policeman arrives. He knocks on her door.

"He's going to move her on," I say.

But no, handing her a coffee and a cigarette he passes the time of day and departs, tipping his hat. We pay-up and leave. Passing her camp we notice smoke exuding from the plughole of the sink. A silvery plume rising in the still air. An ethereal, swirling rope, climbing to the heavens.

Reluctant, ill-fitting legs carry us back to our guesthouse, our minds still entwined in the rising smoke. Incredulity.

"Perhaps we ordered the happy breakfast by mistake?" I suggest.

The End

If you enjoyed the stories in this book by Mark Swain and would like to read other books by the same author, you can find them by searching for '*Mark Swain Author*' on the internet or by asking in most good bookshops.

About The Author

Mark Swain was born in Singapore in 1958, where his father was stationed in the RAF. He has lived in many countries, and as a young man found it hard to break the habit of a nomadic life.

With a low boredom threshold, Mark has had dozens of jobs and quite a few careers. This provides him with endless source material for short stories and is probably the prime reason for the sense of authenticity people see in his work. Studying Graphic Design at Hastings College of Art at 16, he ran off and joined the Army in search of adventure. Later he found himself travelling the world on the QE2 as a silver-service waiter and going to the Falklands war. Training as a TEFL teacher took him to Tokyo in 1984, where he met his wife Lorna. In 2008 Mark took a year out from a career in risk management to cycle 10,000 miles from Ireland to Japan with his teenage son. This life-changing decision resulted in them writing *Long Road Hard Lessons*, which became an Amazon bestseller.

Mark and his wife Lorna have three grown-up children and live in Canterbury, Kent. There is not much in his life that he does without passion, although he will do anything to avoid having to dance or empty a kitchen bin. Asked about his ambitions, desires, or his sense of right and wrong, he says, "I trust in instinct. I simply grow towards the light."

Also by Mark Swain

The story 'Special Treatment', winner of The Kinglake
Short Story Prize, was previously published in Ten
Modern Short Stories 2010 by Kinglake Publishing Ltd

Long Road, Hard Lessons, by Mark Swain (with Sam
Swain). Published 2012 by Tinderbox.
ISBN 978-0-9572002-0-3
Non-fiction book about a father and son's 10,000-mile
cycle journey from Ireland to Japan.
http://longroadhardlessons.blogspot.com

Special Treatment and Other Stories
(Short Excursions into the Lives of Others)
Including the prizewinning story 'Special Treatment'
Published in 2012 by Tinderbox Publishing Ltd.
ISBN 978-0-9572002-2-7
http://sptreatment.blogspot.com